REAL LIFE

Deborah Pease

W. W. NORTON & COMPANY, INC.
NEW YORK

FIRST EDITION
SBN 393 08629 1
Library of Congress Catalog Card No. 78-139385

Published simultaneously in Canada
by George J. McLeod Limited, Toronto
PRINTED IN THE UNITED STATES OF AMERICA

1 2 3 4 5 6 7 8 9 0

FOR NICCOLÒ TUCCI

Contents

Contents

REAL LIFE

1

The First of May

There he was, as simple as that. He crossed the dance floor, his big shoulders in his white suit lifted forward to accommodate the cigar he held in one hand, the drink he held in the other, moving through the crowd of costumed dancers, uncostumed himself. I saw him from the back. His hair was longer than I remembered it. His neck seemed thicker. Uncostumed too, I merely noted his presence. He was here. Al was here. It didn't matter much. I even took a certain pleasure in the disappointment I felt at feeling nothing.

Headley sat beside me, silent beneath his serious mustache, detached in a new, friendly way that made me happy. After nearly a year of floundering about, we had established our friendship, having known for a long time we would be better off as friends. I leaned on the table and gazed over the dance floor. The place was mammoth, some kind of dingy Masonic temple. The rock band played vigorously but couples danced in isolation. There was too much room in spite of the throngs of people and their voluminous getups. On the whole, the party was a failure. A big New York nothing.

Headley, ignoring me in his friendly way, was seized upon by a girl who had been devouring him from afar all evening. Al, the hefty apparition in white, was reabsorbed by the crowd. I forgot about him and the string of non-feelings he evoked. It had all happened so long ago.

"You look the way I feel. Pooped." A voice laughed in my ear. Abigail, my good friend, pulled up a chair.

"Meet Tony. Tony meet Hilary."

"We've met," said Tony gravely.

"When?"

"Just now."

"Is he a jerk or a nice guy?" I asked Abigail, smiling at Tony.

"Which are you, Tony?" she demanded.

"Can't I be both?"

"Tony, your costume is minimal," I said, pointing to the Tinker Bell Is A Fairy button on his otherwise ungarnished dinner jacket.

"Tony is a marvel of irrelevancy," said Abigail fondly. Her concession was a funny hat.

"I'm relevant to myself."

"Lucky you," I said, still smiling.

"Incidentally, why aren't you in a costume?" asked Tony.

"I don't like masquerading," I replied. "I'm no good at playing roles other than the one I ordinarily play."

"And, God knows, that's complicated enough," said Headley in an undertone, without turning around, moving his knee against mine.

I fingered some glasses and lifted one up for inspection. The glass was smudged with lip marks. It held a yellowish intoxicant. I put it down and turned to Headley, who was responding favorably to the attentions of the girl on his right, or so the girl apparently thought, for she pressed ever harder and pretty soon she would press a bit too hard. Her advances would contain just that shade of complacency required to sour Headley's sweetening attentiveness.

"A drink, some corn, and a hot dog, please," I ordered.

"What?"

"You're a lousy provider. I'm sitting here neglected and hungry. If you're going to neglect me, at least you could feed me."

Abigail and Tony left to dance.

The girl smiled ravishingly across Headley and I smiled just as ravishingly back. Our hypocrisy was ritual. We stylized our roles as antagonists. In fact, we liked each other.

"Perhaps you could feed both of us, your two starving females," said the girl, whose accent was roughly Eastern European. Headley wandered off looking for food. Although I liked the girl across the chasm of Headley, I saw no point in bridging the chasm. Nor did I relish the picture of the two of us sitting there like conspirators in his absence.

"Excuse me a minute," I said. "I see someone I know."

And I made my way to the bar, where I knew nobody.

A clamor began onstage. Costumes were being judged. The Master of Ceremonies, wrapped in a polyethylene bag intended to suggest a space suit, tried to rally interest in the proceedings but a defective speaker system and his own bossy manner worked against him. Selected contestants dribbled across the stage and down a ramp in front of the judges. A few people clapped. Most of the costumes needed clarification, nobody could figure them out. The theme was general enough to include any style of dress. A skinny boy with huge diaphanous butterfly wings strapped to his back spread his arms and revolved slowly at the head of the ramp like an indecisive Icarus. More people watched. I moved away from the bar and joined a small group at the edge of the dance floor.

Al passed by and stopped in front of me. His back blocked my view. With the hand that held my cigarette I reached out and tapped his shoulder.

"Al."

He didn't respond but continued to stand there, about to start forward.

"Al?" I withdrew my hand. My voice was high. The boy standing next to me observed my efforts, making me feel foolish and a little desperate. I reached out again.

"Al."

He turned a split second too soon and I knew he had seen me, had been aware of me for some time, and had contrived, probably without admitting it to himself, to plant himself in my line of vision, leaving the act of recognition up to me.

"I don't believe it." He hugged me. He was happy to see me. We separated partially, standing side by side in a half hug, his arm across my shoulders, my arm resting on his back. I had to keep track of my cigarette, which burned close to his magnificent white suit, and, fearing that the ash would fall, smudging the whiteness, hastily withdrew my arm to flick my ash on the floor. He also dropped his arm. I flicked the cigarette onto the floor and he crushed it for me.

"Come, let me get you a drink."

I followed him to the bar.

"When are you going to define your existence?" he asked with a smile as we waited for the drinks.

"Must I define it?"

"Don't you want to, at some point?"

"At some point. But not yet." It seemed to me that my lack of definition dated from that moment in the past when we had permitted a definition to escape us. It was as though Al and I had once owned a splendid bird, a falcon, destined to attain great heights, but in our general reluctance and absence of mind we neglected our bird and shortly, still hooded, it fell from our hands to scratch about on talons near our feet, its expertise belittled into a meanness of beak and claw. Now we made random remarks and simulated closeness as an amenity.

People were dancing again. A girl in a white buckskin jacket with exaggerated fringe danced by our table.

"Too much buckskin," I commented.

"She hasn't got It," said Al.

People passed by carrying corn and hot dogs.

"What is this mania for hot dogs?" I asked.

"It's phallic," replied Al. "Nobody eats the hamburgers."

"What gorgeous girl are you here with?" I asked, testing the extent of my indifference.

"None," he replied wistfully, his eyes allowing their guarded superiority to be replaced by an ingenuous directness. "And you? Who did you come with?"

I glanced around, spotted Headley eating an ear of corn at the caterer's table and pointed him out to Al.

"Oh. I'm not jealous." He grinned, his eyes flickering with their old guile. "Can you have dinner with me tomorrow night?"

"Sure. I'd love to."

"Good. I'll call you. Would you like to dance?"

We danced. In his bigness he was lithe and negligently graceful. Separated by the music, each moving in his own sphere, we shouted across a strip of floor.

"The first girl I ever loved," he declared, giving me his negligent smile as he brought his body close to mine and withdrew at the next beat.

"The same eyes," he murmured, as he took my bare arm and directed me back to the table where Headley sat with a plate of corn on the cob. I slid into my seat and blew him a kiss as he went off.

"No shoes?" Headley asked, blowing through his mustache and the ear of corn.

"I can't dance in them. They keep coming off. What did you do with your Balkan acquisition?"

"I don't know where she went. She got tired of eating corn."

"You treat your conquests so lightly."

"Conquest?"

"What's the name of that Balkan vampire?"

"Balkan? Why Balkan? Why do you want her to be Balkan? What *is* Balkan anyway?"

"The Balkans. Where the trouble starts. 'Watch out for the Balkans,' they always say."

"Her name is Enid."

"Enid. Icky name. Very un-Balkan."

"She's a twin."

"I might have known. Twins tend to have a certain fetal look about them. Big heads. What's her sister's name?"

"How should I know?"

He put down the empty corn ear and wiped his fingers on the tablecloth.

"It's Ibid," he said. "Enid and her sister Ibid."

I embarked on one of my belly laughs over which I have no control and of which I, as well as others, am somewhat in awe. Headley accompanied me with his version of laughter, which was more or less a speeded-up hiccup rendered hirsute in a peculiar way by the overlapping mustache. The two of us, buffalo giggles and hairy hiccups, presented quite a spectacle of mirth to Al, who was pushing toward the exit, his arm around a girl in a tanksuit with balloons supporting tiers of wicker baskets over her head. As he passed the table he leaned down and deposited in my ear the following words: "Until tomorrow, beautiful."

2

Without a Parachute

ABIGAIL CALLED me the next day. "Who was that attractive man in white you were talking to last night?"

"Oh, an old boyfriend. What did you like about him, Abby?"

"I liked his bigness."

I liked his bigness too, I remembered. The way he filled a doorway.

"The first girl I ever loved," he told me again that night. We sat on a banquette, hemmed in by people at a nightclub. The minuscule excuse for a table in front of us was in danger of overturning at my slightest move so I stayed still, pressed against him.

"Then why did you run away? Without a word? I was terribly hurt." I smiled at him. I could afford to smile. The music, the crowd, the encompassing bigness of Al effaced the memory, the concept, the *impertinence* of pain.

He reflected. "I couldn't handle it. I needed my independence. I was proving my independence."

"When you left . . . Shall I tell you what I did?"

"Tell me."

"I called your house to find out where you were and your mother said you had gone to Europe. I kept asking, 'When? For how long?' 'So he left yesterday?' I repeated over and over, like a moron. Your mother sounded so sweet, I wanted to confide in her, but I didn't dare. The rest of the afternoon I spent crying and listening to Ella Fitzgerald. That evening I wrote you a letter, full of accusations, which I never sent." I smiled at him over my crème de menthe. "You didn't deserve all that fuss."

"Seven years," he mused. "Would you like to dance?"

We moved with difficulty out of our corner into the mainstream. I preceded him onto the dance floor and turned to face him. As a matter of course, I slipped into his arms. My left hand, from its demure position on Al's arm, slid gradually up to his shoulder and from his shoulder to the nape of his neck. He folded my right hand onto his chest and held it there. His encircling arm slipped from the middle of my back to a spot considerably lower down, where it remained firmly planted. The music, and our own dancing, was so provocative that we started to laugh.

Within moments, I was falling in love, as I had seven years before, without knowing it. Like a parachutist, I went through the prescribed stages easily enough, matter-of-factly, ascending echelons routinely, getting into position. Unlike a parachutist, I made no distinction between the preparation and the accomplished fact. Believing myself equipped with a parachute to regulate the plunge, I was free-falling through space with no sense of precipitous descent, no knowledge of the bottom or of measures to be taken. Blithely suspended, I took no notice of up and down, of limits, landmarks, or motions to be gone through. At the right time Al, so close, would do what had to be done and together we would billow down from the sky into some divine terrestrial grove, uniquely ours.

3

Safety Pins

HERE THE NARRATIVE begins to disintegrate. There is no way of proceeding directly, in a linear progression, taking events as they come. In general, the last place one begins is at the beginning. It's best to jump right in and commence with safety pins.

He had one of those emergency packets of sewing equipment that they give you on airplanes or in resort hotels. It was in the same top bureau drawer that contained all the slippers you get on international flights. There must have been twenty pairs, neatly stuffed into the drawer. Other airplane goodies also resided there, little plastic satchels and things.

"Do you want some of these?" he asked, magnanimously proffering a dark blue slipper wad.

"When would I wear them?" I asked.

"Now?" he suggested, looking down at my unshod stocking feet. We had been having quite a time on the sofa until the two guests arrived. They were out there now, in the living room, sipping drinks and listening to San Remo hits on the record player. I was unsure of the exact location of my shoes. When the doorbell rang I had such a multiplicity of things to arrange on my person that the shoes were lost in the shuffle. Already feeling slightly sluttish in my stocking feet and rumpled clothes, I had not yet ventured to hunt for my shoes, parting the legs of the newly seated guests to rummage under the sofa. At last Al extracted the sewing kit. He joined his guests. I stood in the doorway.

"Excuse me for a second, will you?" I asked, holding the packet aloft. "I have a hem problem."

"A health problem?" demanded the young man whose name I hadn't quite got. His voice was unbelievably loud and deep. As he was my age, twenty-five, or younger, this booming voice struck me as an affectation. Also, it created an impression of deafness. The escalated volume unnerved me.

"No," I almost yelled into his face. "A *hem* problem. Nothing to do with health, I hope."

"Hem? What is a hem? How boresome." The young man was not an American.

Al sat sprawled in his upholstered easy chair, one compact thigh bulging muscularly over the arm, the rest of the leg dangling, the foot agitating itself lazily. All conversations, great or small, all human exchanges, whether they pertained to undone hems or American intervention abroad, interested him equally.

I withdrew to the bathroom and began mending the hem of my skirt. Given the fact that my sewing skills are limited, I opted for the safety pins, not wanting to spend the next forty minutes incarcerated in Al's bathroom. The safety pins were monstrous, approaching the dimensions of those outsized gold pins we used to wear in our tartan kilts at school. Taking care not to bunch the material, I tried to make the glinting pins as inconspicuous as possible (the whole hem was out, a condition brought on by gymnastics on the sofa). It was not the first time I had found my way into Al's bathroom. I am a great aficionado of bathrooms and Al's was no exception. My affinity for bathrooms has a simple explanation: bathrooms have mirrors and I have periodic compulsions to check up on myself before a mirror. Any bathroom without a mirror is a disappointment and I never stay there long.

I had been out with Al four times. The first night we had dinner and went dancing and then he took me home. The next night we had dinner and went dancing and came back to his place, where I spent the night. The two other nights we had dinner and came back to his place, where I spent the night.

It is worth remarking that the bathroom had two distinct natures, nocturnal and diurnal. In the evening, when I entered it before we left for dinner, the electric light glowed warmly and my face in the mirror looked composed and full of self-confident, if shortsighted and vague, anticipation. Later at night, when we returned, my face would look flushed and lively. In the morning the bathroom suddenly appeared stark and full of defects. The light coming through the translucent glass of the narrow window that never quite closed made everything gray. It was cold. In the tub, the faucet that never quite closed dripped and whined. On the edges of the sink the open razor, the dried blobs of shaving cream, fuzzy with hair like mold, the congealed bits of toothpaste near the drain, the wetness, and the hairbrush, bristles entwined with hair, all reinforced the image of stale grayness I would find in the mirror.

A broken metallic line like hyphens highlighted the hem of my skirt. I was ready to go. The thick pile of the carpet looked luxurious, as did the heavy monogrammed towels neatly folded on racks. Enamel and fixtures gleamed. The mirror of the cabinet over the sink captured reflections precisely, its surface clear and unmarred. My face, poised in that rectangle a second before I opened the door, looked so hopeful.

4

Rhinoceros

When I first knew him seven years before, he had been on the fat side and wore glasses. Now he was no longer fat. True, his name was still Al (the only possible diminutive of Algernon, aside from Algae), and he remained bespectacled, but his corpulence, a major impediment to his perfection, had vanished.

Of what did this perfection consist? Primarily, his effectiveness. At thirty-five he was a successful banker and social figure. His achievements were numerous and much touted. He touted them himself and he was entitled to self-touting, especially as he would never make the blunder of blowing his own horn without dismantling it at the same time. To blow your own horn and take it apart simultaneously is a difficult feat to accomplish. It requires the combined arts of musician and prestidigitator.

Al was part of lots of power structures and his fingers, all ten of them, were in power pots across the nation and throughout the world. Power, contrary to popular belief, is people, not money. In extreme cases, distinctions break down and all three come to mean the same thing. Al handled power-money-people with dexterity, interchanging them, now elevating the values of one, now deploring the venality of the other.

Headley was the antithesis of Al. He was nothing if not brilliantly ineffectual. He supported himself by doing translations from French into English, which was a respectable enough activity except that he rarely got hold of a substantial book, working for the most part on such things as specifications for somebody's yacht, ephemeral tracts embroiling him in the nautical technicalities of bowsprits, bulkheads, and what not.

Once I instructed him in natural history.

"The rhinoceros," I said, "is a large beast with two horns on his nose, one behind the other."

"I know," said Headley.

"Habitually shy and retiring, he is cantankerous if provoked. He eats twigs and leaves, which he plucks with his prehensile upper lip, and roots and tubers, which he digs out of the ground."

"With a hoe."

"He is predominantly nocturnal in habit with poor eyesight but an excellent sense of smell. He is threatened with extinction, like everything else."

"Why are you telling me all this?"

"Would you rather learn how the elephant got his trunk?"

"An alligator pulled his snout."

"If you're such a smarty, I'll discontinue my lesson."

"Discontinue, discontinue, a nonword if there ever was one. 'This line of goods has been discontinued in the same way your life will be discontinued if you don't snap to.' "

"What?"

"He led a long and happy life, full of profits and, at the end, farts. He was a clubman, respected by all, until he was discontinued at the age of eighty-four."

"In spite of his huge size, when a rhino charges at you in your terrorized land rover, what you hear is not a furious bellow but, instead, a teeny squeak."

Headley had been sipping soda through a straw. He removed the straw and pretended to assault me with it.

"Oink, oink," he cried, wild-eyed. "Squeak softly and carry a big horn."

At dinner, Al and his friends bandied about terms like *venture capital* and *hedge funds,* and I dutifully asked what such things were, receiving explanations which I promptly forgot. But I couldn't forget that hedge funds and venture capital and conglomerates and goings-public were real, and squeakily charging rhinos were not.

Al could do anything. He could take mental sprees with rhinos too. It was part of his finesse.

But he never meant it.

5

A Funeral

"You don't have to go yet," he said plaintively as I began my slow climb to the other side of the bed.

"I want to go before you want me to go."

"No. Stay. Please stay."

I straddled him and started to massage his shoulders.

"Who did you take to that party the other night when I couldn't come? A glamour girl?"

"No. A real tough cookie."

"Do you like tough cookies?"

"No."

"Chewy cookies?"

"I like soft cookies."

"Like me? Am I a soft cookie?"

He overturned us.

"You are a soft cookie," he said.

Later, he broke the silence. I never trusted myself with the first words.

"Don't I squash you?"

"A little. But I love it. What about my bones? Don't they poke you?"

"You are perfect. Don't you know you are perfect?"

"When you tell me."

I stayed close to him, fingering his chest, stroking his face, tracing his features like a blind person, reading his body by touch. I looked up at him, committing to memory every curve and declivity; the shape of the nostrils, the brush of interlaced lashes, the texture of his lower lip.

Early in the morning it was best; shorter, less active, but warmer and more relaxed. Some line of demarcation drawn at an imprecise hour of the night served to separate us by daybreak, however, excluding me even from our lovemaking. This invisible boundary was buttressed by the ringing of alarms and phones. All sleep whisked away, Al jolted into his daily routine, full of little attentions to his laundry bag and things.

On weekends, it was laundry bags and out to the country. On weekdays he left early to drive to work, telling me to "get some sleep," which I sorely needed, being a confirmed insomniac. At all times, my presence was an oversight.

In the beginning I spent most of the nights at his place. As he grew used to me, and surer of me, he preferred to come back to my apartment. That way, he could leave when he liked. If, through some miscalculation on his part, we ended up at his apartment, he would take me home, preferring the inconvenience of the trip downtown to the greater inconvenience of waking up in the morning with me by his side. Sometimes he was too tired and I stayed the whole night. This had been one of those times.

He had prepared coffee and urged me to eat the melon in his icebox. He sat on the edge of the bed, pulling on his socks.

"Umm, you smell good," I told him, sitting up and sniffing his cheeks, which smelled of shaving cream.

"My natural fragrance," he grinned. "Fortunately, I am exempt from body odor."

"Hey, could you spare some change, mister? I'll need it for the taxi home."

He stood up, impeccably attired and combed, and looked down at me indulgently. He drew out several coins from his pocket and laughed as he sorted through them.

"This is all I've got. How impecunious of us. Will it be enough?" He put a few quarters and dimes on the bedside table.

"More than enough."

He kissed me hastily good-by and rushed out the door. Tired, but not inclined to sleep, I lay for a moment in bed, sipping the poisonously black coffee and idly contemplating the objects on his bedside table: a lamp, an alarm clock, a radio, and a telephone. All four had one thing in common. They only worked when you turned them on, or activated them in some way. In my weary, speculative mood, what interested me most were the phone and the clock, inanimate objects possessed of a tyrannical inner life.

The black phone, inert and stubborn, reigned on the table like a marvel of taxidermy. Of course, if it rang I never would have answered it, but how many times, in my own apartment, had I walked through the room trying not to look at *my* phone, disbelieving its silence, alert from one second to the next to the possibility of its resuscitation?

My phone was petite and febrile and ladylike. Al's was big and stolid and bludgeonlike. It was difficult to imagine Al sitting all alone by the telephone, as was frequently the case with me, although I sometimes assumed that pose purposely to torment myself. And when my phone *did* ring and when it *was* Al, what stringent control did I exert over myself to keep my voice from shooting out of its normal range, either shrill and high-pitched or hoarsely inaudible. For me, the phone was intimate and surreal, a heightened experience, though not always in the best sense, and what sped along the wire from me to Al was a highly condensed version of myself.

Looking at the phone on the bedside table, I found myself taking a personal dislike to it. It was, after all, for Al, only an instrument.

Finishing the coffee, I got up and walked naked into the kitchen. Opening the icebox, I viewed the usual bachelor contents: cocktail mixes, cheese, beer, soda water, a few strips of smoked salmon half-wrapped in paper, and a casaba melon. With no appetite, I wandered back through the living room, picking up scattered articles of clothing. The apartment was permeated with a gray, discouraging light. In the bedroom I stood before the mirror above the bureau and tried to run a comb through my hopelessly snarled hair. I always end up with rats' nests and about two thousand split ends.

A date book on the bureau-top attracted my attention. Stealthily, I reached for it and was on the verge of examining it when a wave of guilt induced me to replace it. But the temptation was too great. Once a snoop, always a snoop. Tossing scruples to the winds, I pulled open the drawers of his bureau one by one and feasted my eyes on successive terrains of sweaters, shirts, socks, and underpants. I opened the door of a closet and dumbly gaped at suit after suit, shoe after shoe, a million and one ties. Back to the bureau and a glance at the datebook, of a former epoch, chock-a-block full. Then into another drawer, a smaller one, more promising. Pushing invitations and mementos aside, I suddenly found what I suppose I'd been looking for: the picture of a girl, beautiful and not me. I stared at it, seized with paranoia, sure that hidden cameras were transmitting my blatant culpability on a closed circuit TV to Al in his office.

Replacing it, I tried to simulate the original disorder but couldn't remember which odds and ends had been in the drawer and which on the bureau-top. Downfall of a snoop. The datebook alone was enough to incriminate me. I had excavated it from a debris of cards and trinkets now strewn over the bureau. With a sinking heart, I reassembled the puzzle of personal effects as accurately as possible, got dressed, made his bed in atonement, and split from the scene of the crime.

In contrast to Al's penumbral apartment, the day outside

was magnificent, a real spring day. The sky was an untarnished blue with sculpted layers of clouds like sheaves of ice immobile over the green fringe of Central Park. The air was fresh and cool.

A crowd emerged from a church up the street, lots of families, rather dressy. Segments of it lingered near the door at the top of the steps, quietly formal in the bright sun. A portion trailed down the steps in the direction of parked limousines. I noticed, as I approached, the predominance of somber colors and then I saw the widow being escorted to a car. Children followed her and a young girl wearing a wide-brimmed straw hat waited while they bent and disappeared, slowly, into the long black car. There was sound and speech, but the impression was of soundlessness; an aquatic feel to their swaying egress. I walked through their midst and passed the hearse parked at the head of a line of limousines and observed the name of the funeral service mounted in the tinted window and caught sight of my own reflection.

6

All Those Positions

WHY COULDN'T he be a puny commerical traveler in an Alpine hat and a string tie? Granted, under these conditions I never would have loved him, and yet at first I took exception to certain aspects of his appearance and manner. Inasmuch as one has physical preferences, types that recur in one's life, Al was not my type, and never had been even back in the days of my first infatuation. Quite early I'd formulated an image of the perfect man. He was tall but slightly built with a refined face, sensitive features, and prominent bone structure. His eyes, deep-set and melancholy, were the eyes of a poet. He had a thatch of hair tumbling over a high forehead; long, delicate fingers; a deep, hollow voice; a truculent manner concealing realms of sensibility. As I acquired worldly experience I found that many of these poets turned out to be faggots, alas.

Al was a prototype for a nightclub bouncer, even though he didn't engage in that particular activity. Muscle-bound, with narrow, close-set eyes, orderly hair, nasal voice, and spatulate hands, there was no element I could single out and label poetic.

I objected to his foppish habits.

I was insanely attracted by him. Why him and not some-one else? (as a character in a French novel keeps wondering).

"Where do you suppose he learned all those positions?" I asked Abigail over the phone.

"From a sex manual?" she suggested.

"I doubt it. He switches from one to another too expertly."

"In a whorehouse?" she suggested again. "How many positions?"

All barriers were down in this discussion.

"Let's see." I reviewed a series of images. "Maybe ten."

"Ten! Let me think of the ones I know." She began to enumerate:

"The regular one."

"Yes."

"Sideways."

"Um hum."

"From behind. Kneeling and lying down."

"Um."

"Sitting up together."

"Um."

"Sitting up on him."

"Um."

"Standing."

"Um."

"What else is there?"

"Well, ah, Ab, I'm embarrassed to be so clinical."

"Don't be silly. You know we're both fascinated."

"O.K. Well, there's upside down."

"Oh, sixty-nine. I forgot that."

"No, this is where the man lies on top of you but instead of both your heads going in the same direction, his feet are up by your head, and his head is down by your feet."

"I can't picture it."

"I don't like it. I feel alone."

"I should think. Alone with his feet."

"Then there's sideways, not when you're both lying on your sides but when he lies across you so that you form a cross."

"How does that feel?"

"I feel left out."

"What else?"

"Him kneeling and me wrapped around him, in an embrace but with my legs locked around his waist. Then he gets up from the bed with me still clinging to him like a bear to a tree. And he stands up holding me like that, sometimes walking around."

"Wow."

"That is simply unbelievable. Delirious. Then he flings

us both down on the bed. I've never known anything like it." I laughed apologetically. "She speaks from vast stores of experience." I pondered. "I really prefer the normal, old-fashioned position. I love to feel his arms around me and be close to his face. To be intimate. The rest is more impersonal."

Abigail agreed. "You must be very tied to him."

"Terribly. Terribly. And then, of course . . . Well, when it's so perfect, how can you help being in love? How cruel it is, Abby. It's so rare for us and so easy for them. We're so easily seduced. But, at the same time, we're supposed to be liberated, capable of taking our pleasures just like men. It's not the same, just not the same at all. I bet there are very few women who can detach themselves from the physical pleasure they feel, loving the man's body, but not loving the man himself, totally."

"You love Al totally?"

"Everything about him."

"Do you *like* him as well?"

"Unfortunately, yes. He has great charm."

"I don't mean the charm part. I mean, do you approve of his beliefs? He is a big capitalist operator, isn't he?"

"The trouble is that I can't see beyond or under the charm. We're together for such short times and at such intervals. I live more in anticipation of our meetings than during the meetings themselves. Although I hate to part from him, I welcome the moment when I'm alone and can relive the experience at my own pace. It's unreal. It's superficial. But it's also terribly passionate. I accept the fact that I'm going to be hurt in the end, and the end isn't far off, either. From one time to the next I have no assurance that he hasn't decided to drop me."

"How horrible."

"But I'm collaborating, you know. I can't complain. I keep thinking that he loves me too, in his fashion. I make excuses for him. I give him the benefit of the doubt. I spoil him and forfeit his respect. If only I could distinguish between my intuitions and my illusions."

"He sounds to me like the kind of man who knows lots about sex and zero about love; arrogant and defensive when challenged in his feelings. At any rate, you're at a disadvantage making your love for him your whole life. A great disadvantage."

"I know."

"But what about his beliefs?" insisted Abigail. "I bet some of them are pretty shoddy."

"Expedient, maybe, but not really shoddy. Anyway, what's so superior in my existence that gives me the right to condemn Big Money and Big Business, especially since I have a private income? Money and stocks and politics confuse me. The moment I take a positive stand I'm up to my ears in inconsistencies. For example, if you support conservation you know that sea turtles are on the endangered species list, right? You give money to the World Wildlife Fund, you personally boycott luxury items made of tortoise shell or turtle leather, but some evening at a fancy dinner party you are served turtle soup and you eat it because you'd feel like a pretentious bore making a fuss, right? Anyway, it's after the fact, so what's the point. You have given in to the dictates of the situation, you have acted with expediency, you are a fraud."

"Don't be silly. You have acted with a sense of proportion. Your integrity is not impaired, your commitment to turtles is not diminished, and your humanity has not been radicalized to the point of fanatical imbecility."

"All I'm saying, Ab, is that I can't pass judgment. I would like to think that Al is a capitalist pig and an imperialist scab. For the sake of *amour-propre* I would dearly love to feel superior to him, just once, but I'm not that self-righteous. I can't honestly sneer at a capitalist, because I'm benefiting from the fruits of the system as much as he is."

We had strayed from our original topic. We all know that politics and sex are subject to much the same terminology and fraught with similar kinds of power plays. But neither Abigail nor I was, at heart, much interested in polemics past a certain, rather quickly reached point, and besides, just now I didn't want to be distracted from daydreams about Al.

He was away on a business trip, capitalizing. I said goodby to Abigail and leaned back in the chair, closing my eyes and thinking about that wild, clinging, erect embrace.

7

Where Did You Go?

SHORED UP on the edge of that square continent known as Al's bed, with only a scrap of sheet, sleepless, I watched the border of dusk around the drawn shade grow increasingly pellucid. Soon I must go. Like a mountain range, Al divided the continent into two coastal zones. I adhered to the smaller of these littoral strips. No portion of blanketry reached me in my outpost and I had to fight for my scrap of sheet. If I released my grip it would be appropriated by the mountain range in no time flat.

Al's slumber was profound. He rarely changed positions. Now and then he flung an arm or thrashed a leg. Sometimes he sighed, a harsh intake of breath followed by a gentle release. For a second he seemed to surface into consciousness. Before he sank again, out of reach, I turned toward him, touched his shoulder, and said, "Al, I have to go now."

Disturbed, but still not awake, he heaved himself onto his side, wrenching away the sheet. I lay propped up on an elbow and looked at the back of his neck, his shoulders, his impervious recumbency.

It was time to go. Even if my parents, in New York on a visit, had not been expecting me for an early breakfast at their hotel, I would have gone. What was I doing in that bed, all by myself, naked, with no bedclothes? Al possessed everything, even my sleep.

I crawled to the foot of the bed and walked around to the bedside table. The loudly ticking alarm clock read six o'clock. It was a little early to go, but the loneliness of leaving was less than the loneliness of staying here with Al. His face, turned toward me, foreshortened and withdrawn, was the face of a stranger. His ruffled hair, appliquéd upon the pillow in dark crescents, tempted me to smooth it.

I collected my belongings, rummaging through the heap of clothes on the floor like a customer at a bargain basement sale. Last night we had gone to a party together for the first time. We came back to his apartment, joking and gossiping. I took my time, slowly removing my coat, placing it over the arm of a chair, stepping out of my shoes, waiting for him. He put his arm around my waist.

"May I seduce you?"

"I wish you would."

We walked into the bedroom, unhurried.

"You have to undress me. Otherwise I feel like a brazen hussy."

At first, we had removed our clothes alone, in clumsy haste. Helping each other undress took too much time. Now we had reached a plateau and were introducing refinements.

"Umm, how many hooks on this dress."

Later he said, "I'd love to have you spend the night. But . . . perhaps . . . because of your evening clothes . . ." But he had fallen asleep, and although I knew my status would be revised, overnight, from desirable to intrusive, I couldn't deny myself the warmth of falling asleep with him, near him. The minute I was relaxing into sleep, however, something clicked and I snapped into a tense wakefulness, fixating myself on the border of dusk around the drawn shade for the remainder of the night.

Now I stood again beside the bed in my evening dress, a Cinderella who gave in to the prince, all dressed up for last night's ball.

Many of the hooks were unfastened and my stockings had a run. I leaned down and whispered, "Hey. Baby."

Out of reach. I couldn't shake him or shout in his ear, so I left, placing a note on the table in the hall.

He telephoned that afternoon at three o'clock. Usually he phoned in the evening but after a night together he waited a couple of days before calling. I wasn't anticipating his call so I answered not at all in the voice I used in the late afternoon hours when the ring of the phone took on a special note.

Breakfast with my parents had gone badly. The usual bone of contention was gnawed: me. Thinking that one or the other of them might be calling up with a fresh piece of advice, I answered with a *hello* calculated to freeze the blood of any opponent. A pause ensued. My poor parents. I did love them after all.

"Hello?" I repeated, civil this time.

"Ah, Hil'ry." It was Al, it was Al. He always omitted my middle vowel.

"Hello," I purred.

"Where did you go?"

"What?"

"Where did you go last night?" he asked pathetically, like a child.

"Didn't you find my note?"

"No." The tone was defenseless, baffled.

"Oh, baby, I'm so sorry. I tried to tell you but you were sound asleep. I had to have breakfast with my parents. Poor darling. Did you feel deserted?" So seldom did circumstances land me in a position to ladle out consoling words that I got carried away. Two endearments in one breath, and the audacity to think he might be hurt.

He instantly recaptured his normal tone of voice: slow, barely articulated, uniquely stressed, with no unraveling frequencies to give him away.

Al's voice was an instrument so well attuned to the tonalities and requirements of his personality that instead of reflecting his feelings, it absorbed them, like a trombone played with a mute, swallowing the real notes, releasing a facsimile. What sounded affectingly like doubt in his voice, therefore, was *meant* to sound like doubt.

This was a discovery I hadn't made yet, so the sudden change of tone surprised me.

"No, no," he replied calmly, whisking it all away. "No problem. How are you?" We were always inquiring after each other's health.

"So-so?" he answered for me.

"Better than so-so."

"Euphoric?"

"Somewhere in between."

We didn't have much to say. Still, after we hung up, his voice, glazing over the commonplaces, continued to thrill me and I held it to my heart along with that deceptively anxious question, "Where did you go?"

8

Pictures on the Wall

THE WALLS of Al's bedroom were covered with personal memorabilia. Much of this I had examined seven years ago. Photographs of big moments hung all around. The pictorial history of Al Flynn's rise in the world from a fat kid in the Cub Scouts, through the vicissitudes of varsity teams, sporting events, and other people's wedding, to academic laurels, military glory, and invitations to the White House, was herein recorded.

"I can be hard-nosed, but I'm also very sentimental." Al seldom analyzed himself in depth. Confessing my tendency to analyze things, a tendency I resisted but fell into time and time again, consequence of sitting on the sidelines, not even in a front-row seat, I was taken aback by Al's response. He hastened to put distance between us on this score.

"I disqualify, where analysis is concerned. I just don't go in for it."

Although he boasted about his phlegmatic temperament, his laziness, his equanimity, he liked to see himself in strong contrasts, black and white, one moment the hard-nosed businessman ready to "beat the shit" out of a snotty secretary, the next moment a soft-hearted sentimentalist, full of reminiscences.

The crowning enigma, the final touch to this bundle of contradictions known as Al, was the fact that he played the ocarina.

An ocarina is a primitive wind instrument, easily held in the hand, with mouthpiece and finger holes, giving soft, whistlelike tones, on which one can play simple tunes. Whistling away on his ocarina, Al could charm the birds off the trees. He could do that anyway, when he wasn't beating the shit out of them. But the ocarina added immeasurably to his mystique.

Denied access to the mainstream of his life, paddling in a backwater, I never witnessed Al's brilliant moments, but he hinted at them and I could picture them vividly.

Picture a dignitary, dressed in white tie, rising from the banquet table at a formal affair to deliver in witty, well-chosen phrases, a memorable after-dinner toast.

Picture Al at a conference table with a bunch of Latin American associates. The Latin Americans hang loose, wear sideburns, and smoke cigars. Al fits in perfectly. They love him. He speaks their language. They call him Pancho. Their way of conducting business is freewheeling, taking place in private clubs and discothèques as well as in committee rooms.

Pictures on the Wall

Picture a hard-nosed businessman out on the town with a group of salesmen from Minneapolis, fixing them up with prostitutes for the night.

Picture him planting a lettuce garden with the children of an heiress on her Long Island estate.

Picture him conferring with heads of state about economic development.

Add an ocarina.

The ocarina didn't appear in any of the pictures on the wall. The pictures were formal, commemorative. I studied them the way a detective might study mug shots in a police file.

Al at age eight in a group photograph of Cub Scouts. He is fat and squints. His eyes are so light that in this monochrome picture the iris seems as white as the rest of the eyeball. His expression is vacant, the eyes hollow, like the orbital voids of Little Orphan Annie. He looks blind. A radiant smile enlivens the blankness. Al is a happy Cub Scout.

No child, or adult for that matter, is at his best in a group photograph. A regimental sameness, rows of pale ovals on static bodies arranged in horizontal bands one above the other, makes unsmiling faces look grim as death. If everybody smiles at once, the effect is inane beyond description. If nobody smiles, they look like the inmates of some dread institution. If a few people smile one is tempted to wonder, what's wrong with them? If one person alone smiles, clearly he is an idiot.

The smiles were evenly distributed in the Cub Scout photo. Al's smile was entirely normal.

The smile of an adult is frequently a specious commodity, as we all know, but the smile of a child, when unnatural, is immensely sad. It suited my purposes to discern a sadness behind Al's smile. He looked happy, but I knew better. Happy people are easy to understand. I couldn't understand Al. Thus, ran my little syllogism, Al was unhappy, at least as a child, and that was good enough for me. If he was compulsive, or driven, or obscurely motivated, there had to be a key. No key, however, was forthcoming from the Cub Scout picture.

A photo of Al with his army buddies, all smiling in the toughest way imaginable, divulged nothing except a collective ideal of toughness. This toughness was embodied in another picture of Al by himself on the firing range, kneeling and looking down the barrel of a rifle. The picture with its implicit violence disturbed and excited me.

The varsity pictures were unhelpful as far as my investigation was concerned. The athletes stood or sat in their uniforms, in prime physical condition, with short hair and sour faces. They inspired no sympathy and revealed nothing about their humanity beyond an obtuse determination to win.

"I'm a great believer in class and style."

A glance at the wedding pictures and the framed invitations bore out this statement. The weddings were stylish affairs. Al stood next to the happy couple in his top hat and cutaway. He was the best man. Stylish bridesmaids and ushers surrounded the central trio. Al smiled as happily as if he were part not just of the marriage ceremony but of the marriage itself.

Seven years ago, let loose in this gallery of personal

triumphs and treasured memories, my first reaction had been to laugh. It's not *possible*, I chortled to myself, there being no one with whom to share my chortle. People put up pictures of themselves and their friends, that's nothing new. Men hang up diplomas and old school photographs. Girls stick into mirror frames, or under the glass tops of dressing tables, photos taken on the slopes or on elephants. Married couples proudly display pictorial evidence of their affection, unity, and dynastic adjuncts—parents, kids, dogs, and houses in the country. But Al's room was like a retrospective exhibit at a museum in honor of a much-revered public figure, now dead. Girls and family did not figure in the exhibit. They were in the drawer.

Seven years before, we were both in a fluid state. Al was going places but hadn't got anywhere yet outside of the university. His room was in a graduate-school dorm, not in a well-appointed New York apartment. I was going no place. The novelty of my feelings for Al, and his initial reception of them, led me to believe I was unique in his life. In my ignorance, I could afford to laugh.

"You are like a teddy bear," I told him once, late at night. He lay on his stomach in sleepy abandon. I sat on his rear end giving him a postcoital backrub, which I suspected he preferred, at times, to the act of love itself. Backrubs loomed large in our relationship. Every couple has its own code. "Is this good? How is this? Do you like it this way? Tell me, tell me."

"Would you give me a backrub?" came to mean, "Let's make love."

The backrubs in themselves did not constitute *foreplay*,

as that part of the sexual whole is commonly known, nor did they belong in the sector drearily categorized as *after-play*. It amused me to think that Al must have hit upon the backrub ploy fairly early in his career. I could see him as a much younger man, younger than when I first knew him, innocently asking girls to give him backrubs, thereby sailing through the first and most difficult stage of seduction. Once the shirt was peeled away and the torso exposed to view, it was no great distance, psychologically, from the dorsal area to other, more pertinent, areas. True, he still had to take the initiative, the backrub in itself was a dead end. But it was a good way of easing into things.

Needless to say, the masseuse never benefited from backrubs herself, except indirectly. Al would make an effort to caress my back at times, but he couldn't work up much interest in it and fell asleep after a few perfunctory strokes.

Backrubs before lovemaking involved little or no small talk. The anticipation discouraged talk, big or small. Backrubs afterwards were very chatty indeed. I waxed garrulous on all subjects and occasionally found myself talking to a blank back, Al having drifted off to sleep.

Al didn't make much sense during backrubs.

"Listen to the wind," I would say as the wind howled in the airshaft outside my window.

"I have enormous respect for the elements," Al would reply, not trying to be funny, meaning God knows what.

"You're like a great big teddy bear," I told him.

"I like that," he said. "But, you know, someone once told me I reminded him of a professional killer."

"What? Why?"

"I can be very cold."

"You could kill a person in cold blood?"

"If I were betrayed, I could."

"What kind of betrayal?"

"If a colleague cheated or was disloyal."

"A colleague? What about a woman?"

Al grunted. The discussion was taking a personal turn.

Al liked to see himself in dramatic contrasts. The hard-nosed businessman and the soft-hearted sentimentalist. The teddy bear and the professional assassin.

In my unequal position, I couldn't afford to laugh aloud at his pictures and his prideful discrepancies, so I laughed to myself, with inadmissible feelings of tender superiority.

I should have laughed in his face.

9

Invasion of Bugs

ONE NIGHT after he left there was an invasion of bugs, an affliction, like the trials of Job. One hears of epidemics of mice in Australia and sections of the western United States where moving carpets are witnessed throughout the land. On roads, they create hazardous driving conditions. In hospitals, the mice carpets terrorize the bedridden by scampering up the bedposts and dancing on the counterpane.

Luckily, the plague in my bathroom did not reach such proportions. No moving carpet of water bugs was visited upon me. I couldn't help thinking there was something symbolic about their appearance, however. They reminded me, these two bugs, of the toads representing carnal desire in the pictures of Hieronymus Bosch. If they actually had been toads I would have evacuated. As it was, I held my ground.

Shortly after Al left, I got out of bed to go to the bathroom. Pardonable activity. Once in the bathroom, I raised the Venetian blinds to see the night. To my delight, I caught a glimpse of Al crossing the street and disappearing behind some buildings. My heart melted all over again at the sight of him. His solitary figure on an empty street touched me profoundly. I was standing there, being deeply touched, my bare feet growing cold, when suddenly a rush of air streamed over my toes and back again across my ankle. My flesh crawled but I didn't shriek until I had turned on the light and confirmed my suspicions.

Then I behaved exactly the way ladies in cartoons do when they spy a mouse, or a carpet of mice; I jumped up on the nearest chair, the chair in this instance being the toilet. Not having the presence of mind to put the lid down first, I found myself teetering on the rim of the seat in imminent danger of falling into the bowl itself. Meanwhile, the bug, confused by the electric light, froze on the floor, cautiously twitching its antennae. Hysterical as I was, up there on the seat, I felt a measure of compassion for this bug, an empathy insufficient, however, to inhibit my destructive impulses toward it. My problem was to locate and utilize an instrument of destruction. Its problem was to find its way back into the drainpipe. Clearly, it was unhappy in its exposure. One of my fears, aside from my terror of its taking flight and soaring into my hair like a bat, was that it would seek asylum in some cranny and elude me for days. Cohabitation would mean constant victimizing, me by it and it by me. Sensing aggression, it made for the chest of drawers and slipped into a shadow. I sprang, agile as a cat, from the toilet seat and zigzagged to the phone.

"Headley, there's a huge bug in my bathroom. Bigger than a mouse."

"Impossible," said Headley, sleepily.

"*Headley*," I pleaded. "What shall I do? Can you come over and kill it for me?"

"Kill it? Certainly not."

"I know it's against your principles. It's against mine too. But I'm so afraid of it. I can't help it. I'm absolutely petrified."

"Look, Hilary," he began, taking a stern tone.

"Headley, don't moralize now, *please*."

"It's not a cockroach, is it?"

"No. It's ten times bigger. Give me a cockroach any day." All this time, my eyes were riveted on the threshold of the bathroom. If the bug decided to vacate and come in here, all would be lost. I'd never get him.

"See how unreasonable you are? Cockroaches are vermin. Filthy, stupid, prehistoric monsters. Waterbugs, if that's what your friend is, are legitimate insects."

"So you won't come?"

"Hilary, I live at the other end of the city. I'm tired. As it happens, I'm not alone tonight."

"Oh."

"Sorry. That was unnecessary."

"Why be sorry? EEEK! Headley! Here it comes!"

I threw the receiver on the chair and dashed to head off

the bug at the pass. To my astonishment, it obediently shot back into the bathroom. I slammed the door and rushed to the phone.

"Just tell me this, Headley. Do you think bug spray would work? I've got a can of Raid somewhere."

"God, you're inconsistent. You revere life and yet you want to kill a living creature just because its appearance displeases you. You believe in ecology and at the same time you use detergents which muck up the nation's waterways and bug spray that contains deadly poisons. And you're acting like a spoiled brat into the bargain. Think of people in ghettos who have to contend with *rats*."

" 'The nation's waterways?' Headleee, try to understand, why don't you? I spend two beautiful hours with someone I love and then I get a bug in the bathroom." I started to laugh.

"The details of your love life don't interest me. I'll call you tomorrow. Good-by." He hung up. I immediately called back.

"Headley, you listen to me. You have no right to be so abrupt. I wasn't giving you details of my love life. You're still very dear to me, Headley. But I love this man. And I don't know how to behave. It goes all wrong." I began to cry.

"Calm down, sweet. I understand. I'm sorry it isn't working out . . ."

"It's O.K.," I said, defensively. "It's a big adjustment, that's all. Five years of you, kid, is enough to mess anyone up." I was laughing now.

"Go to sleep, angel. Forget brother bug for tonight. I'll come over in the morning."

"O.K., Head. Good night." I replaced the receiver. The situation was intolerable. Big things on my mind and then this God-awful bug violating the sanctity of my thoughts and bathroom. I fished in the closet and finally found some Raid. Then I put on my high-rise Spanish leather boots and flung open the bathroom door. The bug was nowhere to be seen. I sprayed around the chest and after a while out came not one bug but two. The two of them, their dim faculties rendered dimmer by the toxic effects of the spray, dashed in every direction at once. I stomped and sprayed and the three of us created an uproar. In a short time both of them had turned white from several coats of Raid, but neither showed signs of debilitation; if anything, Raid was acting like a shot of adrenalin. Their instincts were screwed up but their powers of locomotion remained intact, even accelerated. Why did they fill me with such dread? Those crazed, forlorn antennae? The crisp, vestigial wings and spiky legs?

Eventually, I murdered them. If there was a lesson to be learned, it was this: Vigilance. Don't be taken by surprise.

I didn't mention the bugs to Al. I would have done so but there was never time.

10

There's No Point

SPRING HAD come and gone. It was the end of June and the blast furnace of summer was upon us. Our affair progressed smoothly. An affair is what it was too, formally speaking. In superficial structure it was an affair. So far, it had acquired no inner dynamism of its own; it did not advance and grow under the impetus of love. Restrictive it was, not expansive in character. After eight weeks we still knew nothing about each other except for a few incidental habits and idiosyncracies. We went out once or twice, sometimes three times a week. We were souls of discretion, taking our time, not crowding each other, allowing countless moments to shed themselves in the belief that infinite moments remained. Those few lost opportunities to clarify ourselves only intensified the thrilling prospect of some future moment of total revelation in which all clouds would be swept aside, our hearts laid bare, gorgeously indiscreet.

Discretion and Indifference. Like two peas in a pod, Headley later pointed out. Hard to tell apart.

A business trip to Europe loomed on the horizon. When Al told me, I asked him how long he expected to be away.

"A week or so. Why?" he asked, looking sideways at me. We sat on his sofa, sipping drinks. I was only there for a drink, it was all the time he could spare. The air conditioner rumbled in the window frame. The apartment was clean, orderly, and smelled of summer in New York, a combination of soot, hot pavements, exhaust fumes, curbsides redolent of crap, and a certain redeeming fragrance, God knows how it survived or where it originated, of real summer, of grass and sun.

"Because," I said, smiling in complicity. We frequently exchanged sly smiles for no good reason.

I wasn't used to affairs. My marriage, or the lay equivalent of a marriage, had protected me from them for nearly five years. It seemed awfully clandestine to me, this affair. We reunited in fits and starts, like adulterers. And we avoided certain subjects, the way adulterers avoid mentioning the wronged party. Only in our case the wronged party had not yet been determined.

The day he was due to leave I called him at his office. His secretary asked if I could wait, he was busy on another line. I held.

"Forgive me for disturbing you," I said hastily when he finally answered.

"No problem."

"I hate to bother you at work."

"No. Why? Not at all."

"I, ah, wanted to ask . . . I was wondering if I could drop by for a second to say good-by to you this evening."

Silence. "Well," he began.

"Just for a minute. To kiss you good-by." Then I added, "I wouldn't be able to stay more than a minute."

"You have commitments," he said playfully, with the peculiar emphasis he imparted to words of more than two syllables.

I relaxed. "Sort of a commitment," I lied.

"I'm in a terrible state of health," he said. "I have a rotten cold. But look, why don't you stop by for a drink at about six? My plane doesn't leave until later tonight."

At six o'clock I stepped out of the elevator and rang the doorbell. Nothing happened. I rang again. Still nothing. He's late. Probably stuck in traffic.

A flight of stairs halfway down the hall offered the only solution. I went and sat on a step, not so much sitting as arranging myself, constructing the scene entitled "Girl on a Staircase" that would burst upon him in all its poignancy when he emerged from the elevator. He did not emerge for a long time. The up and down lights blinked on and off. Together with the grinding of machinery and the slippage of the cables, the blinking disks proved highly diverting. Each time the grinding and clinking and blinking went on for any length of time, I thought, This is it, and consolidated my *mise-en-scène*.

Forty minutes elapsed. Forty minutes draped on the staircase predicting elevators. I opened my handbag and took out a compact. I looked at myself and thought, Little Ass.

When the elevator door slid back, Al exploded into the hall and thrust the key into the lock, all in one motion. A second later the door would slam behind him. The tableau on the staircase was galvanized and fell into disarray.

"Al," I protested.

"Oh. Hil'ry." He opened the door and entered his apartment without looking back. The absence of surprise in his voice told me three things: he had seen me, he had hoped I would be gone by now, he would cope with me nevertheless. Dispirited, I followed him and stood aimlessly in the living room while he threw his jacket on the sofa, snapped open his attaché case, loosened his tie, blew his nose, and headed for the bathroom. Instants later, noises were to be heard.

"Make yourself a drink," he called from the bathroom. The door was open. The first thing he had done was to pee. With the door open. Unprecedented occurrence. I didn't know what to make of it.

I fiddled around in the kitchen, pouring him a scotch, adding the ice, pouring a little more, adding another cube.

"Do you want it while you shave?" I called in to him.

"No."

I held the glass until he joined me in the living room. He sat on the sofa, hurriedly, and took his drink. I sat on the arm of the chair. No loitering. After a sip, he put the glass on the coaster on the table and got up.

"If I drink all that I'll never make it to the airport." Then he stood over me and smiled. All traces of haste vanished. His talent, if it can be specified, lay in his ability to cast off, at a moment's notice, everything extraneous to the matter at hand. Now, for a few seconds, I was the matter at hand.

"Did you get any sun in the park?" he asked, looking at my whiteness doubtfully.

"Only on my kneecaps. No place else."

"And you feel discriminated against."

"Yes, I do," I replied with a laugh. "Just because you're so brown and like to feel superior," I added, relieved to be able to tease him. "It's much more original to be a paleface in the summer."

"There are those who wish to be brown, and those who wish to be white," he said vaguely, mockingly. "Dear me, there's no such thing as status anymore." He ambled to the door of the bedroom. I remained on the arm of the chair, wondering what was to come.

"Wouldn't you like to take a trip too?" he asked with distant concern.

"Where would I go?" I asked, consciously pathetic.

"Where the Beautiful People go." He went into the bedroom.

"I'd rather go where the Ugly People are," I said in a little burst of self-assertion.

"Would you come and help me pack?" His tone was ambiguous. Did he really want me to help him pack or was this another version of the backrub ploy? Did he still have to resort to ploys with me? Playing the game myself, in complete ignorance of the rules, I slid off the arm of the chair and hesitantly approached him. As I drew near I got a look at the bed. From head to foot it was strewn with an incredible litter. Packing was definitely the order of the day. Mortified, I addressed myself to the litter.

Its diversity abashed me: a camera, lenses, boxes of film, tennis shoes, golf shoes, bathing trunks, sweaters, polo shirts, a heap of wide ties, a stack of multi-colored shirts. A bona fide business trip. In order not to leave me out altogether, he consulted me now and then. I advised him on the number of pairs of socks he should take, and which tie would look best with his lavender silk shirt. From an extramarital union minus spouses, our affair had grown, suddenly and without transition, appallingly marital. I was in the unenviable position of the long-suffering wife who stays at home, closing an eye.

Two suitcases lay open on the bed. I folded his evening clothes, carefully smoothing out tails and sleeves and creasing creases. I hung a discarded suit on the wooden clothes stand, but hung it up backwards so he had to change it.

"Oh. Sorry," I said, as he swiftly and without a word fixed the suit. Finally, I sat down on an unfilled corner of the vast bed. He spun about the room, never hesitating, grabbing this and that, flinging soft objects at the bed, fitting them into the expensive canvas bag with leather trappings. It was quite a performance, gracefully choreographed, conducted with a practiced economy of movement; a *pas de deux* in which the prima ballerina sits and twiddles her thumbs.

"I feel very unhelpful."

"On the contrary," he said, stuffing something small into the tight mosaic contents of the bag. "It's helpful to have you here." He was kneeling on the floor now, zipping and strapping.

"I'm going to miss you, you beast," I said, getting up and walking to the foot of the bed, tentatively touching surfaces. He looked up. "I'm unmissable, as they say in the military." Broad smile. As often happened, the innuendoes escaped me. What on earth did he mean?

"You mean you make a good target?"

"There. All done." He stood up. Now he was patting and snapping the other bag. "Why don't you put on a record? We still have some time."

I went into the living room and played the record already on the turntable. It was jazzed-up after-dinner piano music. The first tune was "The Windmills of Your Mind." The simple modulations, like those in elementary finger exercises, made me long for travel and faraway places. I sat on the sofa. The long-stemmed pink carnation I had brought with me as a bon voyage token slipped between the cushions and I was tempted to leave it there, pushing it further under. Little girl with a carnation.

Fortunately, he had missed the carnation. I could drown it under the cushions and he would never know the difference, except that people always do know. They can tell who it is if you phone them and then hang up, and they know if you bury carnations in their sofas. He would disinter it and know I'd left it there. Somehow, it would be discovered. A note from his maid: "Found dead flower." And he'd know.

He dropped the two suitcases by the armchair, picked up his drink, and seated himself, all in one motion.

"Flower," I said, proffering it.

"How sweet of you. Where did you get it?"

"In a store. I didn't pick it in the park." That sounded disagreeably flip. Since he didn't take the flower, I played with it myself, dusting my face with it. In another move he was back in the bedroom, jangling something on the bureau. I followed him, holding the carnation at the end of the stem, letting it sway against my cheek. "Windmills of Your Mind" was reaching a climax. From a glass jar, Al extracted foreign coins.

"Would you like some of these?" He held out some Japanese yen.

"Umm. They're nice. But I don't know what I'd do with them." He reminded me of my father giving me coins he had collected overseas during the War. Perhaps this association gave me a sense of Al's protectiveness that inspired me to ask, childishly, "Al, could I come to the airport with you? I'd just ride out and then come back."

His face snapped shut. Eyes still lowered, presumably fixed on the yen in his palm, he parted his lips slowly. "There's no point. I'm driving out in my car. I'll drop you at your place."

"Oh. I see." I literally recoiled, turning from him and bumping into the clothes stand. I steadied it.

"I thought you might like some company on the way out," I said lightly, straining for composure.

"There's no point. Let's head."

While he replaced the coins in the jar and put the English currency in the pocket of his cream-colored suit, I slipped the carnation into a crevice of the clothes stand, where it would expire, shrivel, and fall to the floor.

We left the apartment. "Windmills" was drawing to a close. The apartment would hear the rest of the blandly impassioned tunes until the record player automatically switched itself off.

He left me and the bags in the lobby and strode down the sidewalk to his car, which was parked at the end of the block. I exchanged pleasantries with the doorman, whose kindness almost made me cry.

"Are you going too, young lady?"

"No. No, I'm not."

I watched Al walking down the sidewalk. This walk was new to me. It wasn't the careless amble with which he entered a restaurant. It was quick and purposeful. He emanated power. I realized that power, and my part in it, was much of what I loved about Al.

"He travels a great deal," remarked the doorman.

Listlessly, I examined the tooled leather of his golf bag. Yes, the golf clubs were going too. My habitual comment on golf has always been, "The shoes are so ugly. Those spikes." My habitual comments are in need of revision.

We loaded the trunk of the car together. I carried the attaché case. He and the doorman said affectionate farewells and the doorman winked at me.

On the corner of Fifth Avenue and Seventy-ninth Street, two girls with long hair and sunglasses waited for the light to change.

"European beauties," observed Al.

"That's a nice beige jacket," I said.

He stopped at my building and we faced each other. His hands remained on the wheel. The motor was running. It was time for me to hurry out of the car, which was blocking traffic. We touched lips, without kissing. He was stalled in an eddy and couldn't drive off right away. When I turned to wave good-by I could tell by his tense profile and the urgent way he bit his nails that my existence had been negated and that his mind was bent on other things.

11

Hanging Around

HANGING AROUND and waiting can be a prudent policy. Lotus seeds in Manchurian peat bogs, after lying dormant for twelve hundred years, bloomed when some thoughtful person planted them in friendly soil. They were patient, those seeds. They knew their hour would come. They prove that those with patience are the best evolutionary prospects. If you are not endowed with exceptional versatility or a high degree of specialization, your best bet is to sit around and wait, like a seed.

Neither versatile nor specialized, my peculiar adaptive feature was an ability to hang around. But, while hanging around involves comparatively little for a seed, it presents something more of a problem for a human being.

By now, Headley knew about Al. When he learned that Al was off on a toot in Europe he leapt, manfully, like the good friend he had become, into the breach, proposing that I drive with him to the Berkshires for the weekend.

We were stuck in a detour on Bruckner Boulevard and already I regretted my decision to come. An atmospheric inversion, blanketing the entire Eastern Seaboard, compressed all families of pollutants, particulate, gaseous, and otherwise, into one insistent fume. I succumbed in the front seat to the fumes, the heat, the whole apocalyptic scene. Droplets of sweat ran down my legs. The innards of the seat burst through the tattered upholstery with the sole intent of persecuting me. Headley's car was an abomination, the biggest vehicle on the road aside from the trucks, a vintage '57 Chrysler, white, with a defective muffler. I kept rolling the window up and down, unable to choose between the heat and the fumes.

"Just think about all that fresh air you'll be getting in a few hours," said Headley.

"Assuming we survive. A month of intensive breathing in the Berkshires wouldn't make up for an hour of this crud."

The driver of the car in the next lane had been staring at me and I reciprocated as rudely as possible. Both our windows were open. Maybe we were going to start spitting at each other, you never know.

"Headley! Hey, Headley!" he shouted. Headley swiveled his mustache in the direction of the voice.

"Oh, Jesus," he mumbled, at the same time baring his teeth in a smile. "Hi, Watson," he shouted back.

"Isn't this *something?*" yelled Watson. A girl next to

him and several people in the two back seats of his station wagon stared at us like chickens in a coop.

"Where you headed?"

"For the Berkshires."

"We're going to the Island. Get in a little sailing on my new sloop. We go out on her so seldom, you know, I figure each sail costs me a few grand."

I wasn't comprehending and wanted to roll up my window, but Watson said, "Who's the girl?"

"An old friend."

"Looks like a young friend to me. Ha ha."

Our lane was moving so we left Watson behind.

"What a creep," I said.

"How do you know he's a creep? He is a creep, but how can you tell?"

"It doesn't take much. Who was the zoo in the back?"

"All his wife's family, I suppose. They get carted around everywhere. His wife is deaf and loaded. At school, Watson always wore double-breasted navy blue blazers with brass buttons and abstruse insignia. I never could stand him." He laughed. "Next week you'll get a call. This voice will say, 'Hello, I'm Watson. We met on Bruckner Boulevard.' "

Aside from this social event, a thunderstorm, and clams at a seafood place, our trip was without incident.

The night was well advanced and dispensing a fragrant drizzle when we drove up the hill to the house. Mrs. Barstow and Headley's elder brother, Jonas, welcomed us into the kitchen. Mrs. B. was a blowzy woman, strangely self-contained and yet continually on the verge of falling apart, focusing on a dozen things at once. Her house resembled her. It rambled, with no apparent center, filled with authentic antiques and worthless knick-knacks.

Headley went straight to his room in the attic without saying good night. Mrs. B. and Jonas and I sat around the kitchen table awhile. The two of them discussed plans for the renovation of the kitchen, which was in an irresolute state, a wheelbarrow full of uprooted tiles in the corner, hunks of plaster all around, shovels and trowels and other equipment hemming us in. Jonas was Mrs. B.'s masculine source of support. Like her dead husband, he forced her to exercise restraint, not always with success.

At midnight, Mrs. B. began to assemble the ingredients for a pie she wanted to bake. Jonas and I walked up the bleached and polished stairs. He deposited my suitcase inside the door of my room and left me. Jonas was a bearded and taciturn young man.

Work was in progress up here too, I noticed. Wooden slats and what looked like shreds of burlap peeked through the sagging plaster of the ceiling over my bed. With some misgivings, I slipped under the bedclothes and pulled the patchwork quilt up to my chin. If the ceiling caved in and buried me alive, Al would know (too late, too late) what a treasure he had lost. I slept little, listening most of the night to a member of the rodent family running across the slats above my head.

On Sunday, some friends came over for lunch and we all sat on the flagstone terrace sunning ourselves and gazing into the smoky valley and at the range of the Berkshires extending in tangible echoes as far as the eye could see. Not a cloud in the sky. Bees weaving through clusters of honeysuckle and drooping fuchsia. The white, wrought-iron table under the grape arbor was laden with a tureen of chowder, bowls of steaming noodles, salad, loaves of fresh bread, and iced tea. Pies were to come, Mrs. B. told us.

Jonas had spent the morning mowing the lawn that sloped down to a field of tangled wildflowers. The smell of warm grass wafted over us. Headley had cultivated the vegetable garden, churning things up with an antique wooden plow. Mrs. B., in between playing Bartók on the piano and working in her flower garden, had cooked up a storm. Aside from banging pots in the kitchen in a display of solidarity with Mrs. B., who knocked herself out with her culinary exploits, all I had done was to hang around.

Our desultory conversation derived mostly from articles in the Sunday *Times*.

"Did you know," Headley proclaimed, "that ninety per cent of the universe is *missing?*"

"Is that so?" somebody said.

I started telling the captive audience about gravity bombs, but this news item excited even less interest than the misplaced universe. Eventually, the subject came around to baldness. Mrs. B. told Jonas she'd seen a much nicer beard than his at the market yesterday morning. Jonas observed that, according to her, his beard was always either too bushy or not bushy enough.

"But what is this influence of yours, child?" she asked in her singsong voice, turning to me. "What kind of effect do you have on these boys that makes them lose their hair?"

The four young men sheepishly returned my appraising glances. All of them were experiencing hair loss to some degree, it was true. Jonas and Headley compensated for receding hairlines by facial growth, but their two friends sported no such accessories. The redhead's hair was thinning at the crown although some scrubbrush helped conceal the incipient bald spot. The other boy, a blond, had hair so lank and sparse that one expected it all to fall out in the next breeze, which it never did, being attached, in fact, quite firmly all around.

"Oh, come, Mrs. B.," I protested, trying to get out of it. "They all have masses of hair."

"But none of it is in the right place," she lamented liltingly.

"Well, we're all bound to lose something somewhere along the line, don't you think? If it's not hair, it's something else, I guess."

"Like our minds," said Headley. "Besides, look who's talking," he continued, turning to his mother. "Your genes are responsible for my ravaged head. You should be ashamed of yourself." Then he sang a little song. "If it's not our hair we're losing, it's our minds, dum de dum, and often it happens all at once, fa la la."

Later, I helped Mrs. B. in the kitchen while the baldies lounged in the sun.

The day before we had set out on a great hike. Jonas and Headley wore mountaineering boots, and I had on some far-out footgear, good for long walks, Mrs. B. assured me. She had her own special prescription for every field of endeavor, whether it involved food, household repairs, or hikes. Like most special prescriptions, they struck anyone accustomed to normal ways of doing things as eccentric, if not insane. She would drive fifteen miles for a special kind of egg, and then fifteen miles in the other direction for a special kind of unbleached flour. She spent hours in the kitchen chopping, pulverizing, and assembling things. Even her cosmetics consisted of special juices and extracts.

The three of us started on our expedition. Jonas pointed out a distant peak as our goal. Headley suggested knapsacks and pitons, but I put my foot down at this (the foot was shod in one of Mrs. B.'s custom-made clodhoppers, a special blend of corduroy, rubber ridges, arch supports, and styrofoam). We clomped across the field, annihilating wildflowers, and clambered over a stone wall wreathed in poison ivy, which lapped at my ankles, unprotected by Mrs. B.'s low-lying gunboats.

"I hate this walk," I announced.

"Be a good sport, and shut up," said Headley.

I could see myself puffed up and blotched with a rash and calamine lotion, welcoming Al back from his travels. We persevered for half an hour through a tame stretch of woodland and then found ourselves on a road.

"Hm," said Headley.

A car approached and slowed down. Mrs. B. poked her head out the window. "Want a ride?"

We didn't answer. Jonas and Headley remained silent out of contempt for the aspersions cast on their prowess as hikers. I fervently hoped she would say, "Get in, I need some help with the groceries," which is what, two seconds later, she did say, and we obeyed.

The only other activity had been a chess game the night before with Jonas, which was inconclusive because when Jonas saw I was winning, he quit.

Before leaving we played croquet. The game ended with everyone shouting, "Oh, sticky wicket," and kicking the wire wickets all over the place.

Mrs. B. was sorry to see us go. Jonas was coming back with us to the big city. He counseled her not to let her enthusiasms go unchecked. We all kissed her good-by. The four of us had been more or less of a family circle for almost five years. I was only recently an estranged member of the unit.

At the end of the long drive, as we neared the city, I moved closer to Headley. Jonas was asleep in the back seat.

"May I drop a pearl of wisdom into your cauliflower ear?"

"Don't cast your pearls into sow's ears," he retorted. "To coin a cliché."

"I advise you not to fall in love with me again."

"Advice already taken. Long ago." He stared ahead, the model motorist. "But what are you doing with *yourself?*" he asked kindly. "Growing up?"

12

More Hanging Around

IF I WAS growing up, it was in a random, weedy fashion having little to do, as yet, with maturity. Much of the obvious still came as a surprise. Abigail made her contribution:

"Al is doing you dirt."

Shocked, I dissected a Hawaiian pineapple ring. We were having supper at Schrafft's. The hostess had shown us at first to a table by the window, where we could participate in staring contests with the passers-by on the sidewalk outside, but the thought that Al might turn out to be one of the contestants led me to veto the window seat in favor of a dark niche by the kitchen.

Slicing the pineapple into infinitesimal slivers, I ruminated. A week had elapsed since Al's return. He had not called me, and the only way I learned of his arrival was by checking with his answering service. A week sounds like nothing, but in addition to the week of the trip itself it meant that for two weeks we had been totally out of touch. He was losing reality for me, which meant that I was losing reality for myself.

He is afraid of involvement was my favorite way of explaining things, implying the reluctant conquest of an overriding passion. I had a mental block: at bottom, it was inconceivable that he might not love me. The premise was: he loves me. The rest of the argument attempted to explain why, if he loves me, does he behave as though he does *not* love me? To support my hypothesis I had evidence. Twice he had told me I was the first girl he had ever loved. Once he had said he was falling in love with me all over again. Once he had proclaimed to the dance floor at large that we were in love, without consulting me first as to my opinion on the matter, evidently assuming that his vote constituted a majority. I was an outvoted minority from the word *go*.

Aside from this evidence, I had other indications of his feeling for me; fugitive glances, half-smiles, touches under the table, the way he reached for my hand, the possessive way he smoothed back my hair. The way we made love.

Headley advocated a direct approach. Call him up. Tell him to stop fucking off. Demand an explanation. Give it to him. Lay it on the line. Have a little self-respect. When pressed, however, Headley admitted that females of this type made most men, himself included, puke. However suppliant I felt, however I aspired to a moral ascendancy,

I did not think much could be gained by making Al puke. So I hung around, voicing no grievances, swallowing my pride, making myself miserable.

Finally I said, "Abigail, if it's true, I don't want to know about it."

"Be realistic, Hil."

"I am realistic. I don't want to be hurt."

"But you *are* hurt, Hilary. Are you going to wait indefinitely for him to call, and then grovel some more?"

"Misunderstandings have to be worked out. It takes patience. I'm sure it's a misunderstanding. Perhaps my aloofness . . ."

"Hilary, come off it. Since when have you been aloof with Al? From what you tell me, *he's* so aloof that you barely get together as it is."

"I may not *feel* aloof, but I don't slobber over him. I try to create the impression that I have an independent existence."

"Look, Hil, he may be a bastard, but he's obviously not an idiot. He knows people. He's canny about them. You yourself say he has an intuitive tact in the way he handles people. That's his specialty. How can he fail to see that you're in love with him? In spite of all your clever ruses."

"My ruses." I hesitated, trimming the fat from my ham steak. "But if it's not a misunderstanding, if I haven't hurt him inadvertently . . ." I interrupted myself. "Maybe I bored him."

Abigail scoffed. "His fault, not yours, if that's the case."

". . . And if he knows I love him, why is he treating me this way?"

"What way? It's the easiest solution. Just don't call.

She'll get the idea. As far as he's concerned, he never committed himself in the first place, so he's not obliged to explain himself."

"He never committed himself in so many words. All the same. . . Abby, it wasn't just a one-night stand."

"A series of one-night stands." Abigail was taking a hard line, for my own good.

Now I was fixing up the broccoli, banishing the stalks. "O.K., Ab. Tell me about it."

"It's something you should know about, Hil. I say this as a friend and not as some horrid little gossipmonger. I wouldn't tell you if I didn't think you were wasting your time on him. You idealize him. You do yourself an injustice by pining over him."

"You talk as if you know him. Did you meet him?"

"Last night."

I stopped playing with my food.

"At a nightclub. I was with Tony, who knows Al. Al came in with a little French number, you know, the tight-blouse-and-slacks syndrome, and they sat at our table."

"Did you talk with him?" I didn't know where to begin. Every detail seemed so important and so irrelevant at the same time.

"Hardly. He was all over this French girl. He couldn't have been less interested in us."

"Did they dance?"

"Yes, if you could call it dancing."

"Abby, are you sure it was Al?"

"Positive. He even had on the same white suit he was wearing at that costume ball."

"Did Tony say anything?"

"Like what?"

"Anything. Did he make any comments about Al?"

"Well, he said that Al was basically a nice guy, but a snob. In the final analysis, you didn't have enough snob appeal."

"I wish you wouldn't use the past tense. It's a little premature."

"Tony also said that Al is ruining himself through ambition. He will be a big success, it seems."

"He already is a big success."

"A bigger one."

"If Tony thinks Al will be a big success, why does he say he's ruining himself? His ambition is paying off."

"You know Tony. He values people for what they are. He doesn't manipulate or exploit them. He thinks Al will lose out in the end by dehumanizing himself."

"I hope he does lose out in the end, and I hope to God he *knows* that he's lost," I said, slamming down my fork.

"Oh, Hil, he's just a playboy. What do you want from him? That kind of man doesn't take women seriously. He uses them for his own satisfaction and vanity and nothing more. He can only abuse you."

"Whew. This quite takes my breath away," I said, placing my shredded paper napkin on the table.

The next day I flew up to Maine to stay with my family and become a child again.

13

Mountain of Glass

DEATH IS always the same, and the death of love obeys the rules that obtain for all other forms of death. Face to face with death, one goes through several stages on the way to a final acceptance; stages that extend over a long period of time, or are condensed into a single instant, depending on the manner in which death overtakes one. The first, universally experienced stage is disbelief.

Perhaps it is overstating the case to draw parallels between my moribund relations with Al and the death of an individual. Considering the degree of fatality involved, there were no similarities. But parallels did exist, in a greatly reduced form, because the process of acceptance was the same.

Not for a single second did I believe Al had dropped me for good. This was the first stage of acceptance: disbelief.

I was early for the ferry and hung about the pier, inhaling sea air. My glasses were back in New York so my visual acuity was much impaired. Maine is frequently fogbound, but I had imported my own fog and now wandered around in the midst of it. A few families, probably known to me but out of focus, got in and out of cars they planned eventually to drive onto the ferry. All the cars in the parking lot, being cars, resembled each other in their essential features, and, insofar as they resembled each other, they also resembled one of their kind in New York, an undistinguished Mustang belonging to Al. Long accustomed to spotting his car, or thinking I'd spotted it, parked or in traffic, I could not shake the habit of spotting it even up here, where common sense told me it would never be. My continued attunement to his car warned me of two things: one, that Maine would do nothing to cure my ailments and two, that a great error had been made in coming up here.

A great error. Up here, there was nothing to remind me of him and so everything reminded me of him. Everything we hadn't shared was here. The loss was here. In New York I had the streets, his building, his car, and every man who, glimpsed from the back or at a distance, might turn out to be Al.

The coast depressed me with its novelty. The ferry, as I stood in the stern looking back across the breakwater, was bearing me away to realms remote from all my reality, and as the gulf widened, the whitecaps erasing the wake, my senses fought against the false nostalgia evoked by solemn conifers on the promontory, the carillon of buoys, the predatory grace of gulls, the scented pressures of the sea, and I felt a childish urge to wave good-by to someone on the distant shore.

There is a fairy tale about a man who, in order to win the princess or flee an ogre, must climb a mountain of glass. Under his own steam, he fails. My mountain of glass was in a molten state half the time, which made the climb painful as well as impossible.

In Maine, when the weather is bad for days at a stretch you lose faith that it will ever be good again. After two beautiful days we were in for four rotten ones, not an unusual ratio, I guess, for any mixture of good and bad, in weather as well as human affairs. The first two days were a trap. I breathed more easily here. Sitting in the sun on the verandah, tacking across the harbor in the sailboat, walking around the cove at low tide—mussel-studded mudflats, wet bayberry, bearded moss, and a new growth of baby spruce—plunging into the icy water, and lying afterward on the warm wood of the dock; these pursuits, although solitary, restored me and lured me away from my mountain of glass.

Then the fog came and kept us inside for four days. What could I do except pace the corridors, recollecting? I didn't know anybody up here anymore. Most people my age were married and someplace else. The huge summer house was like a sarcophagus, replete with moldering memories of childhood.

Mountain of Glass

My parents ran an orderly household. We stuck to a routine and ignored each other, in a nice way.

I would have done a lot of work, reading and writing, but there were too many dead hornets in my room. They lined the window sills and dribbled along the margin of the rugs in the company of exhausted termites and moths; an assemblage of brittle, feathery detritus hindering my mental efforts. Some of the bodies I swept away, but it was a losing battle. New ones kept appearing. The room displeased me. The blind poodle, a faithful family retainer now in his sixteenth year, literally showered my room with his attentions. The poor thing had several old tricks, as old dogs do, the foremost among these bad habits being a propensity for my room. He would take side trips up there from time to time and bump around in some nameless search, pissing at every bump. Had he been an insectivore, I might have pardoned all the discolorations he lavished on my rugs. But he added nothing to the commonweal. My parents loved him, his cataracts, his mite-infested ears, his bladder malfunctions, his eczema, his spindleshanks. They loved him body and soul, and my mother spent a good part of each day applying ointments to his person and popping him pills. For my part, cruel as it sounds, I felt his proper place was in the animal graveyard in the apple orchard. His reward was a long time coming and the sooner it was bestowed, the better. He would get a tombstone along with the deceased horses, abutting the monument to an Unknown Pug.

A good many bees buzzed by the house at all times. The place was rife with insects, and the opportunities to study their various lores were abundant. Hank, the boatman, a bit of lore in himself, had invested in two major items this year: a new set of dentures and a beehive. The false teeth were a godsend. For the first time in years we could understand what Hank was saying. Before, what with the toothless gums, a Down-East accent, and a high degree of reticence, Hank had been unintelligible. His sudden passion for apiculture was less of a general blessing. My parents didn't much like the hive in their orchard, a white box with several thousand menacing inhabitants, but boatmen like Hank were hard to come by, so they put up with it.

Hank was attached to the denizens of his hive in a way that superseded his attachments to his family, his boats, or his lobsters. He took satisfaction in presiding over the bees and their complex social structure. On cloudy days, the colony grew restive, flew hither and thither, was more apt to sting. At swarm time, he told me, they drove out the queen and relocated themselves in, say, a chimney, guided by a dancing scout.

"Not our chimney, I hope."

" 'Tain't likely."

I spent a lot of time with Hank. One morning at five o'clock he took me out in his launch to haul pots. He stuffed severed fish heads in the empty traps and threw back the undersized lobsters. His pots, painted Halloween colors, were peeling and enmeshed in seaweed. The traps, often wrapped in rubbery sheets of kelp, lay close to shore or along far-reaching reefs. I admired Hank, in his yellow slicker, as he patiently inspected his traps, throttling the launch, hauling the slimy ropes, handling the lobsters, baiting the traps, heaving them into the ocean again. He gleaned few marketable lobsters. It wasn't much of a livelihood, but there was a lot of dignity to it.

Our rowboats, the sailboat, and the outboard spent the winter in the boathouse, now empty. When Hank had some free time, he loafed in the boathouse, smoking, or repainting his pots. The boathouse smelled of wood shavings and fresh paint and iron files, dried-out coils of rope, frayed hemp, and the wet canvas of a sail billowing down from the rafters.

I poked through a heap of mildewed *Life* magazines and yellowed pages of newsprint. The drizzle outside, now in its third day, had a timeless character, drizzling past the open door onto the glittery lawn, drizzling onto the rocks on the shore, into the flat sea. An infinity of water falling from the sky into the sedentary water of the earth.

Sitting cross-legged on the paint-spattered floor of the boathouse, leafing through old copies of *Life,* I remembered and re-remembered all of my childhood summers, the intervening winters, the adult summers spent remembering the previous summer spent remembering. I was all remembered up. I had remembered all that formed the matrix of memory. My past was so remembered that I could hardly find my last point on the graph. I had remembered myself out of youth. I had remembered Al. There was nothing left to remember.

Sitting before the fireplace in the big house, roasting my face and watching the flames, was a better kind of boredom, finite at least. Creature comforts deluged me. I ate three, regular, appetizing meals a day, left my room in a mess knowing it would be straightened up (and pissed in), and sated myself before the fire.

I wrote letters and bitter postcards to Al and never sent them. I wrote an unfinished poem apostrophizing the weather:

From what essential gloom
Does my spirit rise
And equate itself with you,
A southeasterly gale on Sunday?

As I composed this immortal verse in front of the fire, my father walked through the room, cleaning his pipe and making noises to help his sinus.

"Gets one's morale down," he said, looking at the picture window, which had been an opaque rectangle for the last few days. "Gets one's morale down."

14

Babies

THE SECOND STAGE in the acceptance of death is false hope, after which comes anger, grief for self, or self-pity, and finally, acceptance itself. Like all emotional states, these levels are not clear-cut and more often merge, now inclining towards one attitude, now towards another. So integral are these stages to a final acceptance of any dreadful truth that they belong together, like notes in a chord which may be played separately or in unison.

I arrived back in New York alternately hopeful, angry, and self-pitying.

One of the first things I did was to go to the Guggenheim Pavilion at Mt. Sinai Hospital, where the daughter of my seamstress had just given birth to a strapping nine-pound baby boy named Vincent.

Madame Alice, a gnomelike figure dressed in black,

waved her handbag at me as I entered the lobby. We stood in a cluster of proud fathers and relatives, waiting for visiting hours to start. Madame Alice, an Algerian, was an excellent seamstress and made special prices for me because I brought her so much stuff to alter, not being a great hand with a needle and thread. We chatted together and she reminisced about North Africa, the orange blossoms, the beaches, and her dead husband. She worshiped her daughter, Madeleine, who had fared rather well in New York, starting out as a translator at the United Nations, giving private lessons on the side, ending up with a pupil who married her and gave her Vincent.

We pushed into the hospital elevator. When the door opened we all poured into the maternity ward. Madame Alice scurried ahead and stopped in front of a pane of glass, behind which stood rows of cardboard boxes, each box filled with a baby, labeled like a plant in a greenhouse.

"*Le voilà! Le voilà! Comment vas-tu, mon trésor? Ô, il est beau! Qu'il est adorable!*"

Vincent squirmed in his box, his eyes open but unresponsive to images. He was bigger than the other kids and had gigantic ears. John, the proud father, joined us at the window and gazed upon his babe. Vincent's squirmings seemed to be in protest of some irregularity.

"He has colic," enunciated Madame Alice slowly to John, who, even though a first-rate father, was a bit of a dunce. He spoke not a word of French except, apparently, *non*.

"*Non*, Mother. He is defecating." John was an earnest young man.

I left the scene of infantile defecation and entered Madeleine's room. It overflowed with plants and flower arrangements and greeting cards from well-wishers. I had brought a single long-stemmed rose of which I suddenly felt ashamed. With apologies, I offered it to Madeleine. She lay in a slightly raised position, looking worn-out. Her delivery had been arduous and she had fever. It made her sad, she told me, that she wasn't up and about like the other mothers, who paid each other visits.

John and Madame Alice and Madeleine and I sat there for an hour, celebrating. We ate sugar-coated almonds. Madeleine told us that the food was good, and the nurses were nice, and that Vincent liked John best. After the first five minutes of celebrating, I was ready to leave. Conversation ran out. Overcome by the boredom of making things up, I sought shelter in a haven of timidity, forcing the others to shoulder the burden, under which they staggered. Stealing glances at my watch, rubbing the petals of a gaudy hydrangea decked out as a rabbit, cringing in my new-found timidity; these were the activities that culminated, at last, in the end of visiting hour.

John and Madame Alice began lugging all the plants and flowers into the bathroom so that Madeleine would not die during the night from carbon dioxide poisoning. I pitched in. Madeleine told us to stop, all the shuffling and scraping was getting on her nerves. I left John and Madame Alice with the new mother, passed in review before Vincent and his confraternity, and, once on the street, took a cab to a Chinese restaurant on upper Broadway where Headley awaited me.

He sat in a booth reading *Time*. I slipped in opposite him and received a twitch of his mustache in greeting.

"Hi," I said.

"Hi."

"Could I see that for a second?"

He handed me the magazine. In a cigarette ad on the back cover, a man resembling Al was lighting up in a blizzard.

"This is what he looks like," I said, showing it to Headley. "It's his type."

"Rugged-looking individual. I thought you said he had short hair. This guy has sideburns."

"Al's hair is long enough so that nobody can accuse him of being a square, and short enough not to offend the clients."

"Do I detect a note of bitterness?"

"A little bitter. Bitter is better."

"Bitter is better than what?"

"Than being a dope. I'm wising up."

"To what?"

"To the ways of the world. To Al. To my pregnancy, maybe."

Headley burst out laughing.

"It isn't *that* funny, Headley," I said, shocked by his levity.

The laughter abated slowly. "I was laughing at the way you said it. What makes you think you're pregnant?"

"My period is more than a week overdue."

"Is that all?"

"But normally I'm so regular. You know that."

"Nothing to get excited about. Big emotions can throw you off. Anyway, what's so bad about a baby? I always said you'd make a beautiful mother."

"That is completely beside the point. Motherhood isn't the point."

"What is the point?"

"The point should be responsibility."

"Yes, I guess it should. But responsibility to whom?"

"To myself."

"My, you are progressing." Headley considered a moment. "Poor little kid. Poor little bun in the oven."

In spite of an impending bun in the oven, I felt relaxed and talkative.

"I just came from a maternity ward. My seamstress had a grandchild. When I see babies with their mothers I'm so envious. Sometimes I think a child of my own would make me really happy. But that's so irresponsible. To everyone. Last but not least, what about the population explosion?"

"A problem indeed. Then you have your darling baby and by the time he's nine he's a radical monster blowing up your basement. Let's think about food."

"Suppose I wanted to get rid of the child," I said in a sepulchral tone. Headley was immersed in the menu. "I don't have the cash. I could never go to my parents. Whenever I ask for extra money just to pay the rent my father gets suspicious. Last time I asked for a hundred dollars he said, 'Hilary, you're not mixed up in a dope ring, are you?' And to tell him I need it for an abortion is out of the question. No, I'd have to raise money somehow."

"You could throw a charity ball," suggested Headley.

Having made me laugh, he proceeded to order just the things I didn't want.

"You don't know what you like, so pipe down and leave it to me," said Headley. "I know this place and I know the specialties."

Headley, mature beyond his twenty-six years in many ways, regressed to his sophomore year in college when it came to judging and selecting restaurants. He had a sophomoric tendency to "discover" the most revolting ethnic eateries and inflict them on his friends, except that his friends usually shared his enthusiasm and would sit around congratulating themselves while the poor girls tried not to throw up.

I looked around the restaurant. The lighting was harsh and dim. The plaster, painted ochre, disintegrated in places, probably crumbling into people's food, adding arsenic to the seasonings. Green plastic Buddhas perched on cornices.

"I wonder how many skinned cats are hanging in the refrigerator."

"Why don't you pretend you're a health inspector and go see?" said Headley, getting touchy.

"There is a distinct dearth of atmosphere. The food must be fantastic," I said, as a bowl of soup arrived. "What's this?"

"Shark's fin soup."

"Where's the fin? All I see is hair. The chef must be going bald. Grease soup with hairs. My favorite dish."

"That is the fin. A fin is fibrous. Those are the fibers of the fin."

"Likely story. Next time somebody complains about hair I'll say, 'Oh, that's just a liver fiber. Liver is fibrous, you know.'"

Headley controlled his temper. He took food seriously and really liked his discoveries. It wasn't merely a question of money. We had always patronized greasy spoons, consuming hateful food that Headley found exquisite.

Shallow as it sounds, Headley's penchant for lousy canteen food and charmless dives was an important factor in my decision not to marry him.

"Cantonese cooking or not," I said, when the grease-soaked dumplings came, "this meal is vile." The barbecued spareribs were adequate, but the lemon sherbet had a piece of cardboard in it. My fortune cookie, hard as a rock and manifestly inedible, spewed forth the heartwarming message: "Many gifts soon." I was getting a monosodium glutamate headache, on the house.

"What if I'm pregnant, Headley?"

"Marry Al."

"Al is no more ready for marriage than a cat. He's a confirmed bachelor. Marriage to him would be a disaster. I tremble at the very thought. But I would love to bear his child." I sighed. "It's so difficult, the whole thing."

"If you *are* pregnant, and you want to have the child, I'll adopt it. You don't have to marry me," said Headley, simply.

Preoccupied with Al, I said, "How kind of you," touching his hand quickly across the table. "How kind of you" was one of Al's phrases. Hearing myself say it, I felt how easy it was to skim over other people's feelings with phrases and adroit touches.

The next afternoon, newly unpregnant, I was lying on the bed in my back room when the phone rang. It was Al.

15

The End Is an Excuse for Another Beginning

SHORTLY BEFORE seven that evening I rang the bell of Al's apartment and stood several seconds staring at the peephole, gaining composure. I reminded myself of a knight about to do battle. He sits in a saddle like a high chair aboard his charger, staring across the meadow at a wall of armor-clad humanity ready to attack. All night he has tossed and turned in his pavilion, scaring himself stiff with thoughts of the approaching battle: lurid visions of arrows winging from crossbows right into his Adam's apple; inconceivable notions of pain and death; general self-mistrust. Now, all he can think of is how one stirrup is longer than the other.

I waited for Al to obey my summons, timid as it was, and when he stood there, the door wide open, his attitude expansive, me still on the far side of the threshold, watching, I moved in two directions at the same time, effortlessly. The first direction was spatial. I moved forward, performing several complex operations all at once. Stepping across the threshold, past him as he held the door; saying *Hi;* propelling myself into the living room; sitting on the sofa—these were my spatial accomplishments.

The second direction was temporal. At one and the same time I was the Hilary who suffered unbecomingly over Al and the Hilary who entered Al's apartment if not exactly with the firm tread of an old hand, at least without the obvious appearance of someone whose heart is beating at three times its normal rate.

But my agitation was remote. I was like a hospital patient whose heart pounds violently enough to shake the bedclothes yet seems to be thumping somewhere else, a thud in the far corner of the room.

My voice was disembodied too. That *Hi* sounded like a phonetics expert in an acoustical booth.

The portable TV was bringing us belated coverage of the moon shot. For the *n*th time we saw the astronauts puttering around their capsule and the lunar module making the connection with its mother ship, in simulation. Al had prepared us both drinks. His informality was catching. He wore slippers. Nevertheless, I was grateful for the TV. For a few minutes we watched the module trying to mate with its mother, in simulation. Al gestured at the screen. "Narcotic effect."

"They should do the whole thing in simulation," I said. "Why bother to go at all? That foolish little module." Very blasé.

"Exactly," he said. He could be so affirmative. "Exactly," he would say, making you feel you had really hit the nail on the head. At times, though, the *exactly*s or *precisely*s or *absolutely*s came too soon, before you had hit the nail all the way in, obliging him to repeat them three or four times until you finished. As a rule, they came in pairs. "Exactly. Exactly."

The narcotic effect took over again, this time with weather and trajectories. Then we were back with the module and its mother.

"Obscene," said Al, referring to the copulating machines. One of Al's talents was his ability to spot the sexual element in just about anything. A legal phrase: Breaking and Entering. The description of an antique table: "The legs are twentieth century," says the dealer. "I'm all for twentieth-century legs," says Al. And if no sexual element was immediately apparent in, for example, a shopping bag full of groceries, he would invent one, saying, "I consume local produce," which, overladen with innuendo, could sound pretty sexy.

Soon the narcotic effect switched to a detergent commercial, which we watched, Al commenting on the housewife's nasal voice, and we were halfway through a laxative ad when Al finally turned it off.

For some reason, we started to talk about death. I'm at

home with big abstractions and generally try to work them in, but just now death seemed intensely beside the point. However, as I didn't know what point he had in mind, and as my own feelings were too unformulated to affix themselves to an exportable point, to a point I could *make,* I pitched in with my thoughts on immortality, which, predictably enough, dovetailed sexily at the end.

I said: "How can you believe in bodily resurrection?" He could have done something with *bodily* but he didn't.

"It's the soul that persists, isn't it?" he asked. Being a Catholic, although rather a poor one, he knew something about church dogma and even attended church each Sunday, "hedging his bets," but he preferred to throw questions back at me unless it was a serious discussion, and we never had those because once we got past the preliminary *exactly*s and *absolutely*s we came to the elephant pit; all the stakes of our antithetical values pointing out of the darkness.

I pontificated a little, ending up with, "But the soul is not a conscious entity."

"No, but it's a sentient entity."

I accepted this and knew it was time to wind up the theology. In the past, our conversations had been preludes, nothing more. I could feel the moment coming when he would put his head in my lap or stretch out his arm. If he made any advances now I was all set to repel them, but I still anticipated that moment of verbal or physical rapprochement, knowing that, in some form, a personal sign was forthcoming and had to come within the next minute, if at all. If the minute passed and still we were bogged down in the church then it wouldn't matter whether I left in ten minutes or two hours because his intentions would have clarified themselves as nonintentions and none of the stress would remain between us to compel me to act one way or the other.

"Are you afraid of death?" I asked, airily.

"I'm not afraid of death so much as I am terribly reluctant to part with life. I have incredible energy. I eat life up," he said, grinning.

We spoke for a moment of infinity.

"It's strange to think of you as a practicing Catholic," I said. He was picking at his thumb. "It adds another dimension to you." But at the same time he said, "Why? Because I made love to you?"

Not sure I had heard correctly I slipped a ring over my knuckle and examined it, waiting for him to go on. The moment had come and it was all his. He captured me with his upward glance and, as he knew I watched him, looked into his lap and played with his drink.

"I could have gone on making love to you, but I felt guilty about it because I wasn't in love with you. Nothing would have been more pleasant than to see you a couple of times a week and make love to you, or turn up late at night to . . ."—he paused, groping for a phrase, and came up with a fairly gross one—"to satisfy your requirements. But I felt that you were getting too involved. I resist domestication, you know. I didn't behave like a shit in not calling you. At least I hope I didn't. My motives, in any event, were what you might call honorable."

He glanced up at me from his slouched position at the

other end of the sofa. His slippered feet were on the table. I stared at him, rapt in spite of myself. I waited. Now he would tell me about the French number. But he had run out of steam. He massaged his glass. I poked at the ice in mine.

"I'd like it if we could be just friends." He glanced up again, through his glasses, his eyes very blue and appealing. Any girl with a grain of sense would have said: "Bullshit." But, wrapped up in a cocoon of my own devising, immured in my own lunar module, I lacked that requisite granule. Far be it from me to insist on my rights, whatever they were. I was not the typical washer-loading, nasal American woman. Oh no. I had the graces and restraints of bygone days and if Al didn't appreciate them, too bad for him. I was patient. No complaints. I understood him the way a moth understands the flame, burning his wings while he waits for the flame to reform its character.

If he didn't volunteer information about the French number, I understood that too. With no guidance from Al I reconstructed the scene to my own satisfaction: Al, wounded by some imagined slight, takes revenge on Hilary by making love to a French number in the presence of Hilary's best friend. Abigail relates goings on to Hilary. Hilary is hurt. Somehow or other, sooner or later, the tensions will be resolved.

Hilary resolved them in her private tribunal where the magistrate sits in judgment on alleged sins, defines the nature of the sin, commits the sin, and becomes the sinner in an attempt to arrive at the fairest possible verdict. The justice meted out in this unusual court of law is exemplary; everyone gets off scot-free.

So I said, "I'd like that too."

Then he reached for my hand, which I did not withdraw.

"When I touch you I still get chills up and down my spine," he said, with another one of his glances. I didn't budge. "How is your love life?" he asked, taking back his hand and looking into his lap.

"I wouldn't call it that."

"Your sex life then." He grinned at his drink.

"That's my business, isn't it?"

"That's your business," he repeated, still grinning.

Shifting his tone and his position, he said, "I've gone in just the other direction. I've been working hard. A real businessman." He never referred to himself as a businessman. Once when he lay on the sofa with his head in my lap, I asked him how he defined himself.

"As a businessman?"

"As a human being."

Evidently he wasn't talking about himself now. He was creating a little image for painless consumption by dopes. He embellished it: "A celibate existence. No women."

I rearranged myself on the sofa. "I'd better go now."

"Do you have to go?"

"I have to go cook dinner for a friend," I lied. It just popped out.

"What are you doing tomorrow night?"

"I don't know yet."

"Would you like to have dinner?"

"Ah . . . No. No, I wouldn't, actually."

"It would be bad for you? Damaging?" he asked, without irony.

I stood up. "I don't know."

"When could you have dinner?"

I had him asking. For the first time since the very beginning he was asking. I savored this particle of power but had no idea how to wield it.

"I don't know."

"Would you want to have dinner, ever?" he asked, getting up.

"I don't know," I replied, smiling. "Call me and see." I put my hand to his cheek.

We waited in the hall for the elevator. Before it descended Al looked at me and said, "You never cooked me a meal." The door began to close.

"There was never time," I answered him.

16

The Necklace

WE STARTED up again. As they say in the trade, once burned, twice shy. At the present rate, I would burn to a frazzle before learning my lesson.

It took me a while to come to terms with the fact that we were permanently stalled and would never get anywhere. We had nothing but beginnings. Like a car whose engine turns over and over generating ineffectual energy but no power, soon we would be flooded and put out of commission. In the meantime, I held this foreknowledge at bay, fighting it tooth and nail.

Without advance notice, he showed up on Sunday evening. We had a tentative date but I had a cold and didn't feel up to seeing anyone, least of all Al, for whom I normally made elaborate preparations, carefully choosing my clothes and taking pains with my appearance. When he phoned I planned to call off our date. At eight o'clock I languished in bed reading a book on psychoanalysis, boning up on my neuroses, blowing my nose, and fitfully removing strands of unwashed hair from my field of vision when the doorbell rang like an alarm of doom.

It was Al, make no mistake. Immobilized by the urgency of doing ten things at once, I allowed the bell to ring several times before I figured out my response.

"Just a moment, Al," I finally called, leaping from the bed, smoothing my hair, grabbing a robe, trying to make my nose less red, turning on some lights so the place wouldn't look like a funeral home. I opened the door. Al filled the doorway with his splendid presence, arrayed in white. He was slow to react, like most big mammals. I loved him for this. You could spill a glass of juice on his pin-striped thigh and while you apologized he would merely observe the stain as it seeped into his trouser. He would bump into things and keep right on going, scarcely noticing, obtusely graceful.

Now he looked at me with somnolent lack of surprise. We both spoke at once.

"You said you'd call."

"I said I'd call, I know."

We walked into the front room, the so-called sitting room. I led the way, angular and unarranged. At moments, I threw myself on his mercy, playfully, but with a kind of desperation. I clung to him and said, "Oh, Al, you look so nice, and I'm so awful." I accentuated my awfulness with a sniff. He was so big and reassuring, letting me cling to him, the real pioneer man of my dreams, Honest Abe back from a day of splitting rails.

He held me loosely. "You *feel* wonderful."

We sat on the sofa and drank fortifying mixtures of vodka and bouillon. My self-consciousness ebbed. It was useless to worry about my present flaws, there were too many of them: dirty hair, pallid complexion, runny nose, unshaven legs, broken nails, boarding-school shortie pajamas (the satin and lace negligees lay among lavender sachets, neatly folded in the bureau drawer), a chintzy Chinese robe, and a pair of turquoise stretch bedroom slippers that some evil-minded person had stuffed into my Christmas stocking once upon a time. Having nothing to recommend me beyond what I could salvage of my personality, I made do with that.

"It's good of you not to run away. I'm such a hag tonight."

"Not at all. You're a friend who's feeling bum. I wouldn't run out on you."

"You're a big believer in friendship, aren't you?"

"Absolutely. Aren't you? I'd walk a mile for a friend."

"I believe in friendship but I'm not too good at it. Basically, I'm only loyal to people I love."

Al shrugged, "Love. Like. What's the difference?"

Here I felt I had the edge. In discussions of subjective states of mind I had the edge over Al, who didn't waste much time on such peripheral issues. Riding high on my moral credentials as a Feeler, I said, "The difference is qualitative, not just a matter of more or less. Liking is liking and loving is loving, to be succinct."

"The molecular structure of love puts it in a class by itself? Something pure, removed, extraordinary . . ." He grinned at me.

"Pure, removed, extraordinary," I repeated, smiling at him but steering clear of implications or avowals. We got off on another tack.

"You have so many friends. How do you keep up with them all?" I asked.

"My biggest problem is laziness. I could spend all my time with friends and never get anything done."

"You seem to combine business with pleasure pretty well."

"After a while all my friends begin to seem irrelevant."

"Irrelevant? You mean expendable?"

"No. Just irrelevant." He looked up through his glasses. "Unless you're in politics. Then they all become voters."

Like many men in their thirties with a good education, social connections, competitive drive, and a certain eminence in banking or law, Al had toyed with the idea of going into politics. A whole segment of his generation at college was grooming itself directly or indirectly for various elective or appointive seats of power.

Politics was a subject dear to Al's heart and never far from his mind. He loved to talk about politics. Since I met Al I had learned to read the paper. Virtually anything newsworthy was grist for my mill. A collection of phrases pertaining to world affairs flowed glibly from my tongue. I worked up an interest in putsches, bloodless coups, nationalized oil fields, Great Leaps Forward, austerity drives,

Middle Americans, Retirement Communities, cryonics, missile silos, cyclamates, Consumerism, juvenocracy, Food Stamps, effluents and sludge, military homicide, preventive detention, protective reaction, habeas corpus, Inner City, infrastructures, numbers rackets, geodesic domes, residential patterns, recycled waste, nonrenewable resources, irreversible trends, botulin bullets, Torrey Pines, cybernetics, broad-based coalitions, vehicular emissions, coal-tar derivatives, sensory overload, situation ethics, environmental din, hog cholera, balance of payments, Gay Power, contour farming, cantilevers, plankton, macrobiotics, leathercraft, cosmic rays, data banks, Billy Graham, inflationary spirals, and garbage accords, and so forth and so on.

Now I ate an apple and acted girlish, twisting off the stem and denting the skin of the apple with it, assigning an initial to each twist and each attempted dent, coming up with the initials of my future husband. My future husband, lucky individual, what on earth would he be? A Bolivian tin king? A household-poisons magnate? A stone farmer on the Outer Hebrides?

Al and I stayed away from subjects like marriage, husbands, and love. Once, to set him at his ease, I said, "I'm never going to get married."

Chomping on the apple, I waited. We proceeded in fits and starts like the propulsions of water spiders, suavely intermittent.

"I have a present for you," he said. I made a gleeful face and waited some more. He pulled from his pocket something wrapped in tissue paper. His presentation touched me. A token of affection! I had never received one from Al, and I attached great importance to it.

He watched me unwrap it. A necklace of three strands of beads glazed in mottled earth colors. It wasn't exactly my taste and I would probably never wear it, but it was very precious to me. Solemnly, Al accepted my gratitude.

"How does the clasp work?" he asked. "Is it too stiff?"

"No, no. It works perfectly." I fastened the necklace around my throat and displayed it to him.

"It's quite nice," he said. He leaned towards me and kissed my throat, my ear. I intended to resist him, and tried to, but always with Al I never thought beyond the next two seconds.

"I want you," he murmured. "I want you desperately." To achieve a tactical advantage over him should I have repulsed him then and there, delivering a speech on respectful behavior towards women?

We lay against each other on the sofa, silent a long time. The sad aftermath when he fell asleep and I presided over that deathfully inserted distance did not occur, partly due to our cramped position on the sofa and to the fact that he was fully clothed, but due also to a new, gentler awareness between us. He kissed my nose and forehead, non-erogenous zones. We brushed eyelashes. We were solicitous about each other's comfort. He was going to get contact lenses, he said.

That was a poor idea, I said. When he removed his glasses he looked vulnerable. With contacts, with everything in focus, he would look invulnerable all the time.

"I'll always be vulnerable to you. You have such a hold over me."

"Um hum."

"You don't believe me?"

"You like to say nice things. I know you, Al. I'd like to believe you, but I don't. Nope." But I did, of course.

17

Fantasies

For years, people have been saying, "Hilary, you really ought to do Something," and I have continued to perform variations on the theme of Nothing. The thematic material has worn pretty thin at times, I'll admit. One had to have a genius for sloth to live the way I did, constantly a prey to fantasies that were the imbecilities of a brain saturated in idleness, bubbles on the surface of a mire, a slough, a viscid bog.

Lying on my bed in the back room of this apartment, I daydreamed about a Yak. They shot him at midday, just across the street. I watched from the bathroom window. Mild-mannered while alive, posthumously he caused a lot of trouble, holding up traffic and creating quite a disposal problem, which they finally solved by shoving his carcass into the back of a sanitation truck. I had been watching passers-by, picking up fashion ideas, when hard on the heels of a maxi coat came this Yak (*Bos grunniens*). Despite his considerable size, he moved with dexterity along the sidewalk. He refrained from littering the street with droppings even though back home in Tibet his do-do served the community, people burned it for fuel. Here they burned fossil fuels, he knew. He didn't know much, though. He tried to imitate the average pedestrian, window shopping and keeping to himself, but the cops came in their squad car and fired their pistols into his shaggy face as he stood at the curb waiting for the light to change.

Yak, Yak, never again will you see your migratory pastures in Nepal or delight the peasantry with your droppings. Patient beast of burden, your mortal remains are bobbing bloated out past the Statue of Liberty.

The Yak scenario didn't lead anywhere, so I had another one ready, this time about death by drowning. I imagined what it would be like to stand on the deck of a transatlantic liner at night in mid-ocean and to jump overboard. First, the enormity of a realized impulse, the sheer shock of doing it. Then, the breathless, regretted plunge. Then the icy impact and flailing for the surface, for coherence. The sealed fate, the involuntary shouts of panic, the churning stern, the lights; the well-regulated entirety of the ship is still so close. Figures blot out lighted portholes. You and the ocean and the vessel are still of the same medium, undifferentiated.

The sea is flat calm. The ship is on an even keel. Shortly it regains itself, recedes, is no longer eclipsed or bound by inchoate elements of night, noise, and the generation of power. The beaded lights twinkle in the distance. The noise, the forward movement, the bulk of the ship are reintegrated. You are alone, outside the wake, which foams with a sizzle, in a freezing darkness of one global substance. Your panic aborts itself, like a fishbowl over your head. You tread water, insane with the thought of the fathoms of teeming ocean beneath you. The ship shrinks in a nimbus of blurred light.

Glad to be safe and sound in my own apartment, I got up and boiled an egg.

Al would never say, like other people, "Hilary, why don't you *do* something?" But one day he said, in his elliptical way, "Don't you think it's good to be involved? To help people?"

"Yes," I said, and within two days I had three jobs on my hands. I had plunged into the maelstrom of human activity. My metabolism underwent profound changes. My fantasies assumed new, more topical proportions. I was a working girl at last.

18

Job Number One

MONDAY through Wednesday in the mornings I helped oversee a bunch of black kids in the basement of a nearby Episcopal church. They came downtown from a day care center in Harlem, boys and girls aged six to thirteen. Accompanied by two or three older black girls, they streamed into the church each morning at eleven, whereupon it became our job to divert them until two. At that hour, guided by two or three adults, the kids went for a walk in the park, or to a museum, or to a municipal swimming pool. Since my other job began at two thirty, I missed these afternoon jaunts.

Sam, a recent law school graduate turned teacher as a means of avoiding the draft, was in charge of our sociological operations. He received a salary. The rest of us were volunteers, inept but eager to help out.

"Improvise," said Sam, my first day on the job.

The teaching paraphernalia was more than adequate, considering our amateur outfit. Sam, efficient and resourceful himself, was married to a school teacher, who suggested most of the stuff we used; mimeographed worksheets and texts, and shiny pamphlets of reading matter with simple stories and bright illustrations.

I liked the idea of working with these children. They were lively, appealing, and did not intimidate me as I had feared they might, unaccustomed as I was to kids. But aside from lending moral support to the enterprise, I failed to see how my untrained efforts were going to benefit anyone.

Fortunately, the general situation was not critical; it was too unstructured to permit of failure. The program, if it could be called that, didn't aspire to much beyond keeping these kids occupied for a large part of each day. The instruction was incidental.

Nevertheless, we plugged along, trying to inculcate whatever we could that might be useful. Sam brought in fresh supplies of worksheets, crayons, and gold stars every day. The stars devaluated speedily, pasted on foreheads and chins, as well as on papers less than one hundred per cent correct. Often the worksheets were overambitious. Homonyms and antonyms were over everybody's head, volunteers included.

The kids changed as well as the personnel. One day fifteen would arrive and behave like angels. The next day twenty-eight might show up and the result was fights and stampedes.

After an hour or so of the classroom routine, we watched movies. Every few days I exchanged old films for new ones at the public library. Most of them showed how Africans lived. Some depicted shanty towns in the southern United States. Others showed wildlife on the great preserves in Kenya. Still others were mistakes, which we sat through anyway. The kids weren't fussy. It was much the same to them whether they saw Masai warriors or a convention of midwestern homemakers, except that the African films had good music which the audience couldn't resist, and most of the shows ended up in a burst of animation, with assorted limbs intercepting the projector light, creating a show of their own.

Sandwiches, milk, and candy were distributed at one o'clock. As the day drew to a close, many missiles filled the air, crayons, bread crusts, chalks, erasers, shoes.

During the movies, some of which were lengthy, the collective attention span fluctuated. Brenda, the chief rabble-rouser, sat behind me with her cronies and quizzed me about my love life. They fooled with my hair and wrapped strands of it around their pencils. Sometimes they got pretty rough and before I reached the point of raising my voice one of the older girls would tell them to cut it out. Charlene, about eighteen, believed in corporal punishment. She whacked and screamed and laughed and taught with equal vigor. When we played games, she was the foremost participant. She knew all the songs the kids sing when they jump rope and could do all the tricks.

I would get in there and mess up with a regularity that delighted my pupils. They showed me how to run into the arc of the rope without tripping over it but I never got the hang of it. I tried to blame it on them. The rope-swingers, being a third my size, did not describe a sufficiently high arc with the rope. I got it in the neck every time. But they wouldn't listen to my excuses.

"Ha, Ha. She messed up again." My authority, never a strong point, was undermined, but they all liked me, even Brenda in her own diabolical way.

Johnny appointed himself my boyfriend. At first it was rather sweet, but I soon began to feel it was inappropriate. A gangling youth, thirteen years old, belligerent and affectionate like the others, he purposely misinterpreted my rejections. Seated next to each other at another blooper of a movie, this time about dentists, Johnny put his head in my lap and made goo-goo eyes at me while Brenda and her crowd commented loudly from the back row.

"Ooooh. Teacher's got a boyfriend. Are you going to kiss her, Johnny? Ooooh. Have you ever been kissed, teacher?"

"Brenda, shut up," I yelled. I was catching on fast. "And Johnny, sit up. Come on. Right now. Watch the movie." Charlene threw me an approving glance and I felt proud of myself. Approbation from Charlene was not easily won.

"But it's about dentists."

"Well, sit up anyway. It's almost over."

Parts of the audience dispersed, ran around the room, out into the hall, down by the bathrooms, always a popular spot, through the room again into the church kitchen, back into the room, and onto the stage, where they danced the boogaloo until they were too tired to do anything else but watch a bunch of orthodontic surgeons.

The decibel level in the basement rose to an unheard-of pitch and in no time flat one of the ministers rushed to the door.

"Sam," he said in a lugubrious tone, "there is a funeral going on upstairs. We can hear you down here. Please, please, keep the children quiet."

When the kids heard this, all hell broke loose. Disrupting funerals was more fun than dentists any day. But Charlene, in bellows that conceivably might have been overheard by the deceased himself, took charge and order was restored. Johnny, as good a funeral disrupter as any, was off and running during the apex of the commotion but now that things had calmed down he took notice of me again. He entwined his arms around me and rested his head on my shoulder. I almost said, "Be a big boy," but realized he was behaving like a big boy already and didn't need further encouragement in this direction. Brenda and the fans were going wild in the back row. I took Johnny by the shoulders and placed him upright in his chair.

"Sit up and behave yourself, Johnny. I'm not kidding."

"You don't like me because I'm black," he whined. It wasn't the first time I had run into this. Most kids knew they had this card up their sleeves. Kids are never honorable opponents and resort to any cheap trick, as well they might when confronted with the subterfuge of adults, but I wasn't going to let him get away with it this time. Smiling at him, I said, "Johnny, that's a lot of shit, and you know it. Come on, let's clean up this mess."

The dentists gone, we all faced the garbage dump on the floor, pushed it into piles, and tried to sweep it into receptacles. After two minutes the cleanup squad turned into another brawl, and the debris was getting pushed by big janitor's brooms in every direction but that of the wastebaskets. Sam came down hard. He got very mad at everybody. After ten minutes the place looked less like a battlefield. Sam gave us some workbooks to check over for the next morning. We arranged the sheets, crayon stubs, and broken pieces of chalk on a shelf.

"If you have any new ideas . . . ?" Sam always asked, hopefully. But my colleagues and I were barren of innovation. We left it up to Sam, the professional among us. Discipline was discussed. Fewer kids was the answer. It was two o'clock and the kids were raring to go.

Charlene, outside on the sidewalk, was breaking up a group accidentally terrorizing a passing poodle. Out in the sun, the kids looked gay, small, and oddly needful. Unaffected by the heat, protesting another museum trip, hungry again, and docile in a column behind Charlene and Sam, the little regiment straggled down the sidewalk. I stood by the door and waved to them.

"See you tomorrow."

After a morning of being roughed up by the kids, I felt battle-scarred and ready for trouble. Al liked the idea of my involvement with black kids. He was on the bandwagon of negritude himself as an adviser to a job-training program for dropouts. It gave us a new subject of conversation. Al enjoyed the image of himself as a civil libertarian, although he never made the gaffe of taking his social consciousness too seriously.

One of Al's more endearing qualities and notable social graces was the leeway he granted others for fatuous remarks, creating this license by the number of platitudes he himself uttered on any given subject, provided the cliché was currently fashionable and not instantly recognizable as such. I made this wicked observation to Abigail.

"Before ecology became a household word, Al never gave it a thought. Now he's the first to talk about permafrost."

"What's permafrost?" asked Abigail. "A new kind of frozen orange juice?"

"It's what might melt when they lay that pipeline in the Alaskan tundra."

I did wish, however, that Al could have seen me in action with my kids. I came on strong, smacking and hugging and improvising with a decisiveness I never showed with him. Strangely enough, I never bothered to understand these kids. We had an equilibrium; we acted and reacted. Our resultant interaction was spontaneous. There was nothing to lose, on either side.

19

Job Number Two

Mondays through Wednesdays in the afternoons, I worked as a file clerk in an organization with the unfortunate acronym of SOG. The initials stood for Scientists' Organization Group, an unedifying title. Nothing about this group, from its titular peculiarity on down, made much sense to me, undoubtedly because I had a fish-eye view of its workings in my capacity as file clerk. They had pamphlets and brochures explaining what purpose they served, but ten minutes after I'd informed myself my memory failed me and I simply could not remember what we did or account for my presence with this group. We kept enormous amounts of information on file. In this respect I was an important part of the bureaucracy. We also sent our form letters announcing breakfasts at the Roosevelt Hotel and lectures at institutes, and every now and then we published a magazine called *Ecological Imperatives.* SOG was a worthy, unaffiliated, nonprofit organization with far-reaching influence and some prominent activists and scientists on its board of directors. It subsisted on foundation grants and contributions from members.

At the top it was as official as anything official ever is. At the bottom, where I resided, however, not much worked.

When I joined up they promised me I could help write a newsletter, but until some funds materialized I would have to bide my time as a file clerk, hiding my light under a bushel of clippings from the *New York Times,* the *Congressional Record,* and many periodicals. Incidentally, none of the funds allocated to the newsletter would be diverted to me: I was a volunteer worker at SOG. Nobody could believe my dedication to the cause, particularly to a cause so hard to define.

Naturally, I played down the file clerk bit. Al, Headley, and Abigail all thought I was working on this newsletter, shrouded in mystery, coming from Hades for all they knew. My parents, stunned by my collection of jobs, tried to enlighten themselves about SOG, but failed, and concluded that I was working for a subsidiary of the CIA, sending out newsletters to interested parties.

Marta, a Yugoslav about my age, who wore butterfly eyelashes that peeled off at the edges and were so heavy she could barely keep her eyes open, let alone bat them (nobody to bat at here), showed me around. We worked in the same room, she at a desk by the window and I at a long table near the wall. Each afternoon I arrived to find a new pile of clippings, neatly pasted up and dated, on the table. On days when the chief paster and clipper had better things to do, the chore of cutting out relevant news items fell to me. There was a huge backlog of unfiled stuff, and the files themselves were a shambles. My predecessor had a fondness for the miscellaneous file and had invented another heading, when the miscellaneous drawer overflowed, entitled *general*. All the other files bearing more specific captions were nearly empty. I was meant to straighten up the filing system.

It was fun for a while, like kindergarten, sorting things out, making little piles, cutting, pasting, shuffling articles from one manila folder to another. Marta envied me.

"I love that kind of work," she said, leaning on her typewriter. "The best job I ever had was selling postcards at the Metropolitan Museum."

Marta worked part-time at SOG, devoting most of her energies to a dissertation on Comparative Anthropology. She received a salary and had a title, Director of Scientific Affairs, which she claimed was grandiose and inaccurate and sounded too much like a dating service. We agreed that I deserved a title too, but Chief Bureaucrat, although apt, lacked dignity. Most of the letters that she typed had to be signed by a scientist as well as by Marta, and when a scientist was unavailable, I signed, forging ornate, scrolled signatures. I became the Special Assistant to a Letterhead.

Marta had a number of little phobias, none conducive to productive work. Her main problem was an inability to finish anything. In graduate school, she explained, the termination of a thesis and a love affair had occurred at the same time and traumatized her to the point where she could not bear to come to the end of anything. She got sick as she approached the last lines of a form letter.

"I'm going to be sick," she would say, cheerfully. Then she persevered for a few more words and, sure enough, would make an egregious error. After some halfhearted attempts at erasing the bungle, she gave up, overjoyed at having to tear out the letter and begin anew. Whenever she managed, after sickness and erasures, to get through an entire letter, the result was exceedingly unprofessional. All our form letters, sent to hundreds of highly placed subscribers, bore the signs of Marta's traumas; blots, gaps, and hybridized letters not to be found in the alphabet of the English language—capital *O*'s transformed into *P*'s, lower case *b*'s forced to be *v*'s, and so on.

One day she placed a stack of Xeroxed announcements on the window sill and a zephyr lifted half the stack out the window. The sheets wafted down into a construction pit and Marta spent the next hour batting her butterflys at the hardhats and watching them drill through the memoranda.

Periodically, she gave forth data about herself and the old days in Yugoslavia. She would rest her elbows on the typewriter keys, conveniently squashing some gibberish onto the page, and say with a faraway look in her eyes, "When I was a little girl I put a raw pea up my nose and my mother had to get it out with a hat pin."

The trouble with news items was the tidbits on the reverse side. On the back of a report on vehicular emissions was part of a supermarket ad. Marta, with her passion for the incomplete, always read the wrong side of my clippings.

"Hmm. Something or other shell steaks at something something price per pound." She reflected on her findings, "Shell steaks. I didn't know they were crustaceans."

Aside from Marta, work at SOG was pretty dull. The name of the game, the big, overall game, was Ecology, but the name of my game was Drudgery. The spirit of the law, so to speak, was admirable and of the first magnitude in importance, but the letter of the law, as practiced by me, was infinitely tedious. I found it difficult to persuade myself that I was a vital cog. Cog or no cog, the issue boiled down to whether I felt useful at SOG and I did not feel useful. It is true that my usefulness was of less concern to me than the effect of my multiple job-holding on Al. So far, my activities proved to be a breath of fresh air between us, chiefly as a talking point but also because my rushing about animated me, imparting a vitality I had lacked until now. The vitality was superficial, the taproots extensive but close to the surface. Anecdotes, personalities, points of comparison now supplanted random experiences and the figments of my imagination.

20

Job Number Three

ABIGAIL HELPED me land my job at The Store. The Store was small and tasteful and catered to those who liked good contemporary design in everything pertaining to the domestic environment. The bias was Scandinavian, with a faintly elitist appeal. But the work was not elite. Poorly paid and often grubby, it was little like working in a prestigious sweatshop.

Abigail was in charge of the lamp department at The Store. Her real work, freelance fashion illustration, didn't pay well enough, although she commanded rather high fees, so she supplemented her income with lamps. They were masterpieces of industrial design, these lamps. Occasionally their prototypes turned up at an exhibition at the Museum of Modern Art.

Thursdays through Saturdays I worked at The Store,

at first as a receptionist and later as a salesgirl. If my activities with the kids and my filing with SOG helped infuse new life into my one-sided relationship with Al, my performance at The Store was geared to obliterating Al altogether. I was so unsuited to my work there that if I swerved from the strictest attention to the details that threatened to overwhelm me at every moment, I was overwhelmed.

Al welcomed his obliteration. He hated the idea that I might be mooning around, daydreaming about him. All my little chores and dabblings in the fine art of retailing were meant to dilute my obsession with him. If I thought about Al while making change, I would shortchange the customer. And if I failed to banish Al's image from my mind while taking calls, I ran the risk of disconnecting a big buyer, which happened even when I paid attention. But Al's picture of my activity was highly schematic. His involvement with his work guaranteed that for at least eight hours a day his personal life would be pushed into the background. More often than not, the public life, the courting of clients, spilled over into the other hours as well, completely negating the private life. He enjoyed his work and was very caught up in it.

My motivation, on the other hand, had nothing to do with the work I chose to undertake. It had everything to do with Al, and since my efforts to put distance between us were really a means of achieving greater closeness, every step away from him led not in the opposite direction, but straight back to the starting point: Al. Instead of making clear distinctions between my private and public life, utilizing the one to set the other into sharper relief, turning from one sphere to the other with a sense of refreshment and change, I made a colossal blur of any distinctions, not content to keep my personal life in abeyance but compelled to drag it with me everywhere, right into the midst of commercial transactions. Not surprisingly then, at the end of the day when most people reorient themselves from work to play I had nothing to orient myself towards or away from, and came home just as disoriented as when I got out of bed that morning. Al was always in my mind, in the background or at the forefront, but always there.

They started me off as a receptionist because I had no sales experience and possessed an outward demeanor not calculated to drive people screaming out the door. You couldn't just sit and answer the phone, however. In the first place, the phone wasn't that easy to answer. If you are not acquainted with office life you are not likely to know about all those buttons, especially that ominous Hold button. When three extensions ring at once, flashing their little lights, what you are meant to do, the manager told me, is to push each one of them, politely but speedily saying, "Hello, please hold," subsequently consigning the caller to the oblivion known as Hold, an oblivion we all hoped would be temporary but which sometimes lasted forever.

After a rash of calls, some redeemed from Hold, some not, a second generation cropped up, spawned by the Hold button.

"You cut me off," said an angry voice.

"Whoops, so sorry, please hold," I would say, punching it out of my life to answer a second call.

"You cut me off," said the second caller.

"Oh dear, please hold," I would say, punching twice and liberating the first one.

In the second place, you weren't allowed to sit around. The entrance hall adjoined the main floor known as the Accessories Department, which dealt in pots and pans renowned for their good design and colorful appearance. The girls were kept on their toes by the floor manager, years younger than myself, who saw to it that I kept on my toes too.

Abigail sat at a lamp-strewn desk on the mezzanine and when the manager was out of earshot she called down bits of advice. When the manager went out to lunch or left early, Abigail came down and sat in one of the kiddie chairs on rollers, ingenious Swedish design, that rolled about the entrance hall.

"The big ethic here is 'Don't hang around.' Look happy, busy, fresh as a daisy. It isn't enough to be busy. Just answering the phone and taking messages will get you fired in a week. Got to be dynamic."

"How much more dynamic can I get? I rearrange my desktop constantly. I water those chrysanthemum plants so much that the water runs all over the floor. I mop it up and water them some more. Keeping busy. Killing the plants. I'm always tinkering with the stuff in the display window and sweeping up imaginary dust. I do little dances to the music. If I get much more active up here people will think I have a nervous disorder."

Job Number Three

Kneeling in front of the window stenciling a message on the plate glass about the goods on display (mounds of Finnish basketball sneakers, orange and aquamarine, selling for a price that ensured The Store a seven hundred per cent profit on each pair), I was an object of curiosity to passers-by. They smiled in at me and I smiled back. The heat was in no way abolished by the air-conditioning system in the building, which cooled only the top two floors. The mezzanine and the main floor, while not oppressively hot for the customer who didn't dawdle, were stuffy and humid and all the salesgirls were smitten. I was having the worst time of all in the window under the blazing display lights and in the magnified glare of the sun. I wore a smock of heavy cotton with no shape whatever. Several of these smocks hung in the window. The smocks were functional house dresses and permitted great freedom of movement to countless hordes of Scandinavian housewives, but mine, one of the staff dresses we all shared, although roomy, hampered me at every turn.

I knew that Al would never pass in front of this window and look in upon my sunny diligence, but I smiled at them all anyway, with a certain hopefulness. A man halfway down the block had a forehead that sloped like Al's. Another man, crossing the street, carried his shoulders like Al. Still another, approaching the window with a kindly interest in its melting mannequin, had a face which, in the configuration of its lower half, the long jaw, the severe mouth, the straight, thin nose, resembled Al's.

The man looked at me through the window. I avoided his eyes and concentrated on pressing the stenciled letters onto the glass. He studied me and I glanced up but the glare brought tears to my eyes and forced me to look down quickly. He moved to the door. His figure in the doorway was much smaller than Al's. His body did not fill the frame.

"I thought at first you were a model, but then you moved," he said in a pleasant voice. His attention made me uncomfortable. He stood just inside the door watching me in profile. I acknowledged him with a small, vexed smile. After a few seconds I turned to suggest he leave but the moment our eyes met he smiled, reached out to touch my cheek, and said, "You're beautiful." Then he walked away.

21

A Lot of Existence

SUMMER WAS not a peak season at The Store. Abigail had plenty of time for her fashion sketches. Aside from lending out lamps to be photographed, there was not much doing in the lamp department.

The girls in the furniture section took turns reclining in the Naugahyde-and-cherrywood lounge chair and trying out the trundle bed.

The Store hit the doldrums. The dog days were upon us. The ship was becalmed and unsold merchandise hung around our necks like so many albatrosses. Idle salesgirls outnumbered idle customers five to one. The girls could have perfected their sales techniques, but they didn't take notice of a customer unless the manager was around. They sat on the counter, legs dangling, and sent out for orders from the drugstore. The counter was lined with foodstuffs. After a while, you forgot you were working in a business enterprise. It didn't seem real. I answered the phone with my mouth full of tuna fish.

Annette gift-wrapped parcels down in the stockroom, an unwholesome place. There wasn't much gift-wrapping to do so she spent her time dusting off the shelves and coming upstairs for air.

"Get married," said Annette. Recently married herself, she found marriage the ideal solution and advocated it for everyone. "Get married. It's the only thing."

"I will someday, I trust."

"Do you have someone?"

"Yes, but not for marriage."

"That's all a waste of time. Life's too short."

It's all a matter of how you define Real Life, I decided. For Annette, love was not Real Life until consecrated by marriage. For me, so far, nothing was exactly Real Life. The Store was not Real Life, and neither was Al. The Store was life in miniature, trivialized. Al was bigger than life, inflated all out of proportion. And I floated somewhere in between.

Life at The Store, trivial as it was, persisted in a real enough fashion in spite of the doldrums. Fabrics had a mild traffic. As we all had discounts, we were tempted to browse and smell out any rare bargain before it could be discovered by a customer. Although the discounts made for small reductions unless you bought in bulk, the fact that you could buy an item for less than the retail price was a powerful inducement to purchase almost anything, whether you needed it or not; particularly if you neither needed it nor liked it. Helena, in fabrics, always noised it about when a good-sized bolt of material was going into the bargain barrel. Even without a bargain, the fabrics were a drawing card for personnel. We bought swatches and turned out our own dresses and skirts to vary the daily uniform of staff dresses. I never went in for couture of this type, not being a great hand with needle and thread, but I got Helena to whip up a skirt for me at a low price.

Most of the shipments arrived on Monday. Abigail, who worked part-time every day, was on the look-out for things that should be snatched up. She exercised her judgment in the matter and set many goodies aside for me when I came in on Thursday morning. Three dozen Italian wine liters covered the Hold shelf in the basement in my name.

"Abigail, are you out of your mind?"

"Don't you like them?"

"I like them but what are they for? I don't run a brewery."

"They're selling like hot cakes."

That was the rationale; if it sells it must be desirable, so buy it up first and find a use for it later. The display team loaded my desk with liters so it fell to me to extol their virtues to customers dubious of their uses. I improvised.

"Oh, you can use them as vases, for one thing. Put in a peacock feather, very charming. Also, they can serve as martini shakers."

"What about a top? They don't come with a top. How can you mix a drink in a bottle without a top?" demanded a shrewd customer.

"You cover it with your hand. That's how they do it in Italy."

Since they were inexpensive, the only cheap articles in The Store, people bought quantities of them. In a couple of days they were sold out and we had to place a new order. I ended up with a few myself, although not three dozen. It was difficult to buck a buying trend.

I bought lots of little gifts for Al but didn't dare give him most of them. I did give him a Danish Fish Chart, without which no Danish bathroom is complete. I also presented him with a brass Super Egg in a suede pouch. When it became clear that my largess embarrassed him, I stopped.

Often I wondered why, if he loved me seven years ago, didn't he love me now, when I was so much better? It was my conviction that at the age of eighteen I had been a malleable nincompoop with room for much improvement. In my modest evaluation of myself, I had improved beyond anyone's wildest dreams.

Five years with Headley had shaken a lot of nonsense out of me, for although we had lived in a world of our own and were extrinsic to certain functional realities, we were nevertheless in touch with these realities and maintained a wobbly orbit despite pressures to zoom into outer space.

"You're not sophisticated," Al once said, "but you've had a lot of existence."

Wasn't I a better person for my existence? My existence had not been a salient feature when I was eighteen. At that juncture in my career I had accumulated little beyond a frantic willingness to flirt. Flirting made normal human relations unnecessary for the time being.

I compared my present twenty-five-year-old self with my former incarnation and tried to see what he found so lovable in me then, and what element was missing now. Time had eliminated a lot of nonsense, though not all by any means. Presumably, the nonsense alone had not captivated Al, but eighteen-year-old nonsense was forgivable. Now that I was older and wiser, to behave like a girl of eighteen was absurd and yet, discounting my present charms since they didn't seem to work with Al, I clung to what had worked in the past, although nothing could have been said to work very well even then. No wonder things were in such a mess.

22

The Nozzle Crisis

"She's new here."

"I'm new here."

Once I was made a salesgirl, these two sentences found frequent utterance. Secretly, I knew that no matter how long I stayed at The Store, excuses would dog my steps. After six months they couldn't go on saying, "She's new here." They would have to fire me or come up with something else like "She's a mental defective," or "She's no good." I could hear myself saying, "Please accept my apologies, I'm just no good."

The job at The Store was defeating all its purposes. My rich supply of anecdotes did not amuse Al, mainly because I was the butt of them and he saw nothing funny about incompetence. Also, while Day Care and Ecology were impressive banners to fly, work as a lowly salesgirl was, in his books, if not something to be ashamed of, at least nothing to brag about. The fact is, none of this made a particle of difference; whatever activity I chose was beyond the scope of our affair, adding nothing of substance, only taking up time, wearing me out.

Supposedly, I was making it easier on myself, keeping busy, with a life of my own. In fact, each job strained my resources and all together they exhausted me, leaving me no time to touch base or collect myself. In mid-August, barely a month after our reunification, Al went away on a business trip to the Far East. When he returned, after Labor Day, the summer program at the church had ended, I had quit SOG and was whittling down my job at The Store. During September and October I worked a few hours a week at The Store. Before Thangsgiving, I quit.

In the meantime, we had a nozzle crisis and a blender heist.

An article in a weekly magazine decrying stores in which salespersons didn't know the first thing about the stuff they were pushing inspired the manager to crack down. Several machines, pertaining to food, manufactured in West Germany, lined the lower shelves, defying anyone to work them. They were intricately designed, aesthetically pleasing, and expensive. If we sold one it boosted our tally at the end of the day and everybody felt good. Customers liked these white, plastic, clean-looking machines. They liked all the tricks the machines could perform: grinding, squashing, mashing, splitting, slicing, grating. But they hesitated to buy one because, in spite of the booklets that analyzed each part in great detail and portrayed heaps of groceries before and after, none of us could give an explanation that made perfect sense. Approximate sense we could manage.

"Well, you stick the apple in here, see, and put the top on. Then you switch it on and the juice comes out this nozzle."

"You put in the whole apple?"

"Maybe you'd be better off removing the core. Also the skin, I guess."

"But an apple wouldn't fit, would it?"

"You'd have to cut it up first."

"Wait a minute. This attachment isn't for apples. It's for coffee beans."

"Oh, yes. You're quite right. The apple attachment is down here. Osterizer. It osterizes anything. Carrots, pencils, fingers . . ."

If you could get them to buy the whole works, with all the attachments, the accessories department took a new lease on life.

One day I sold a juicer. A few days later the man who had made the purchase stopped by to report that he had lost the nozzle and would like another one. I asked Manuel in the stockroom if he knew the whereabouts of the nozzles. Manuel said either you take a nozzle off a new machine, invalidating that machine, or you send to West Germany for a new one. Not averse to wrecking a new juicer for the sake of a customer's well-being, I checked the machines in stock but the only juicer left was without a nozzle and also had a crack. Abigail would put it on the Hold shelf in my name one of these days.

After my hunt for the nozzle, I began to fill an order for six five-piece place settings of Rosenthal china. The thought of sending to Germany for a nozzle went clean out of my head and the nozzle question got quietly dropped.

A week later, I was on the phone with the customer whose order of china I had filled. She had received a shipment of china which, by some oversight, was not the china she had selected and paid for. As the facts revealed themselves and we checked the receipt, it became clear, to my mounting horror, that not only had I sent out the wrong china but I had undercharged on two additional items, omitted the tax on a hundred dollar purchase, and sent out part of a back order that had already been sent. Trying to sound unperturbed, I jotted down information and blamed as much of the mess as I could on the boys in the shipping department. The woman listened patiently but, at heart, was not interested in why it went wrong but only in when it would be fixed up. In all candor, I should have told her to cancel her order and place it at a department store down the street which sold the same china at a more reasonable price, because if she stuck with us she would not get satisfaction, for the simple reason that it took a mind differently constructed from mine to get to the bottom of these wondrous miscarriages.

Lacking candor, I said none of this and was reading back to her the ins and outs of her case, when I noticed the nozzle man hovering by the cash register waiting for me to hang up so he could ask me why he didn't have his nozzle. As I couldn't dream up a good reason, I kept my customer on the phone longer than necessary, filling her ear with drivel.

Finally I faced him. "Ah, yes, you are the gentleman who requested the nozzle to the juicer. There are none in stock at the moment and we do not expect a shipment from Germany for a few weeks. I believe there is a store on Forty-third Street which sells parts to this machine. If you like, I will find the address for you and instead of waiting you could . . ." I put on a Swedish accent, hoping to intimidate him.

He broke in, "I bought the juicer here and it's up to you to replace the nozzle for me. I don't have time to run around the city looking for spare parts."

"Yes sir, I understand. But you will have to be patient. We will send you the nozzle as soon as it arrives."

"How many weeks?"

"About six."

"Six weeks! That's outrageous. The juicer doesn't work without the nozzle."

"I realize that, sir, but we did sell you the complete machine. You were the one who lost the nozzle." I was dying to ask him how he managed to lose a nozzle. He left in a huff, and the question once more got quietly dropped.

23

The Blender Heist

ABOUT A WEEK later, a young man shoplifted a blender, pride and joy of the accessories department. The Holy Grail.

It was early in the afternoon. Abigail and I were getting set to go for lunch. I wrote up a sales slip and handed the customer her purchase in a shopping bag. As I put the money in the cash register I caught sight of a young man headed toward the door with our blender under his arm. A thought ran through my mind, *That young man is walking out with a blender under his arm.* Abigail, waiting on a brightly colored high chair by the phone, grabbed my arm and whispered, "That guy just stole your blender."

She was off in hot pursuit of the man who, the moment he reached the door, broke into a run. I followed her and the two of us ran down the sidewalk, Abigail shouting, "Stop, thief!" People turned to stare, wondering where the cameramen were. We apprehended the felon at the street corner. The light turned green and the three of us crossed together. Abigail, for all her hue and cry, was now mute.

"Excuse me, sir," I said, trotting to keep up with him. "Where are you going with that blender?"

He stared at me in amazement, without breaking his stride.

"I'm taking it to show my wife," he replied.

"Ahh . . . Did you pay for it?" I asked timidly, getting worried. Maybe he was innocent.

"Of course I paid for it."

"Could you show us your sales slip, please?" My presence of mind broke all records.

"Nobody gave me any sales slip," he growled, stopping abruptly. "Look, I bought this blender. Nobody gave me a sales slip. I'm taking it to show my wife. Would you leave me alone?"

He spoke with difficulty and his eyes didn't seem to focus. His appearance was unkempt and his manner urgent. Drug addict, I thought. But, God knows, with our unparalleled margin for error, he might have bought the blender without anyone knowing about it. Abigail gawked and offered no assistance.

"O.K.?" he demanded.

The matter was out of our hands. What authority did we wield, two girls in smocks?

"O.K." I agreed. Abigail looked shocked.

"Hilary, you let him get away," she reproached me on our way back to The Store.

"*I* let him get away. What about you? You're a fine one to talk. Big help. 'Stop, thief,' my eye." We giggled.

A small crowd stood in front of The Store, on the sidewalk. Most of it consisted of salesgirls. Some of it consisted of onlookers. One of it consisted of the nozzle man.

"Oh, no. It's him." I stopped dead in my tracks.

"Who?"

"The nozzle fiend. I can't see him. He must know that I never ordered his nozzle. Look, he's conspiring with the manager. I bet she checked it out. Abigail, let's duck into the Deli."

"But they're watching us."

"Never mind. It's our lunch hour."

"I have a better idea. You go home and call in sick. I'll go back and fill them in on the heist. Someone else will have to deal with the nozzle."

"Say the shock was too great."

"I'll say that."

"Ab, you're a fine human being."

The next day I called in sick again, just to be on the safe side. It had been quite a little episode. I could hardly wait to tell Al.

"Al, the funniest thing happened at The Store today." We spoke on the phone. Over the phone we had our most successful conversations, from my point of view, because I literally had his ear. On the other end he might be opening invitations or reading *Women's Wear Daily*, finding fault with the way I dressed, but this I could not know, nor in fact did it ever occur to me that I had anything but his undivided attention. Over the phone we gave and received in a form of communication limited to the voice and the ear. Our eyes and smiles could not come into play. His voice, even through its mutes and stops, was unavoidably direct. If controlled and impersonal, it was still on exhibit. He was on auricular display. I recorded the vibrations of his voice the way a seismic device records disturbances beneath the earth's surface. And I was conscious of the tremors within myself as together we listened to my voice. The pronunciation of a single word, a single vowel, the tone and shape of it, influenced me for hours afterwards. I would remember his words, and mine, and their confluence.

My funny story didn't lend itself to vocal subtleties or seductions, but it insured me smooth sailing for several minutes. I was greatly taken up with the Blender Heist, which seemed to me hilarious. As I got deeper into the story, I began to receive little waves of incomprehension from the other end of the line. The trouble was that Al took shoplifting seriously. It was a kind of pathology, or social ill, or retail dilemma, not susceptible to humor. Not funny. Nothing funny about money. If I had told him the story to illustrate a point, say, on why The Store ought to employ a security guard, he might have shown interest. He did show interest in the heist but not in the humor I was vainly trying to wrest from it.

"It really was awfully funny," I concluded, unrewarded by any laughs.

"Stores have to figure shoplifting in the price of their overhead," said Al.

Oh, Al . . . Al. Al. Al.

24

Luminous Dial

He wore a diver's watch of stainless steel. Rustproof, shockproof, waterproof, self-winding, with disks and subdivisions, a black face, luminescent numerals and hands, it was a bulky timepiece and he usually removed it when he neared the vicinity of a bed, his or mine. I divested myself of my jewels, such as they were, rings and earrings. A necklace, posing no threat other than possible strangulation, could stay where it was, but bracelets and baubles, protrusions and sharp edges, had to go.

One night in late October the watch was no longer just a watch but became for me a kind of sad talisman, siding with me against its rightful owner. Since Al's return from the Far East in early September we had seen each other with some regularity, once or twice a week, but always with the slate wiped clean, nothing carrying over from one meeting to the next. He persisted in identifying himself each time he called, as though I were an acquaintance who might have difficulty not only recognizing his voice but in remembering him at all. Tabula Rasa Al, starting from scratch each time. Two or three times in the last months he had asked me my age. He would grin and say, "Are you nineteen?"

Grinning myself, I would say, "You know how old I am. I'm twenty-five." But the longer we knew each other and continued not to know each other, the less sure I became that our little routines were a joke. They were not a joke; he simply forgot. Al and I could not stay at the beginning forever, asking each other's names. We had already had our second beginning.

"Off again, on again, gone again, Finnegan. My mother tells this story about an Irishman and a train. At the end, Finnegan sends this telegram: 'Off again, on again, gone again, Finnegan.' " I was leading up to something, a mild diatribe, but I couldn't launch it because I forgot the rest of the story, and also Al had fallen asleep. I lay by his side, staring at the ceiling. After twenty minutes or so I got up to turn off the lights. Al woke up.

"Hil'ry, I have to go."

He reached for his watch on the bureau and fastened it around his wrist. I left the lamp on across the room and walked back to the bed. I slipped in beside him hoping that he would want to make love again. Nestling against him, I waited. He propped himself up on an elbow and continued to fasten his watchband. The watch was a complex mechanism and the band itself, links of stainless steel, had a security snap. Al was having trouble with the security snap. His back was turned, but I clambered partway over him to inspect the operations.

"*Difficile*," I said, tumbling over his side and lying on his arm. Playfully, I helped him put on his watch by taking it off.

"What are you doing?"

"Helping out," I laughed.

"I have to go. Really," he said, almost crossly, unmoved by my antics. It didn't occur to me to ask why, and he didn't offer to explain.

Awkwardly, I freed his arm and lay still. He snapped the band on his wrist and tried to sit up but fell back onto the pillows for an instant and went to sleep. Again I stared at the ceiling. Again I got up to turn off the light. Al stirred and mumbled. Halfway across the room, taking care to be quiet, I stopped, surreptitious and absurd and angry. He made me feel I was keeping him there against his will. I turned off the light and went back to bed. Creeping under the covers, I lay close to him again, my head on his outstretched arm. Wide awake, my anger mounted. As the night wore on it changed to sadness and then to a loneliness suffused with longing for Al. But where was Al? This form, adamant against me, would wake in a few hours full of energy, anxious to repudiate the night and rush into the day.

The luminous dial on his watch was more alive to me than Al. I stared at its face next to my cheek. The second hand traversed the numerals in a staccato swing and lay coupled for an instant with the mint green hands of the hour. The movement and the glow took on an existential significance. Trapped under the shatterproof crystal, time was deprived of virulence, like scorpions in clear plastic medallions on key chains; fossilized like ants in amber. I couldn't take my eyes off the watch. As long as I kept it under surveillance, time swam harmlessly around the dial, a swift silhouette without dimension. And I was without dimension, or a place in time, which meant that the night, however lonely, would never end.

25

Running Around in Circles

"THERE IS a symmetry in nature and in natural law," said Headley. We were walking around the reservoir in Central Park. I had expressed the vindictive hope that, if there was any justice in the world, Al would come to a bad end. Headley answered me indirectly, elevating the discussion to a higher plane.

"Any concept of justice ultimately is based on this natural balance. Leaving aside the administration of justice, taking justice pure and simple we ask: 'Does it exist? Is there such a thing as Divine Justice? Retribution? Heavenly rewards for the Good, and damnation for the Evil?' The point is always nature. Religious and mythological notions of justice are based on nature. Everything in life, in human affairs, in matters of the spirit finds a correlation in nature. There is a sublime and simple discretion in nature. Justice and goodness exist in the simple fulfillment of natural roles and needs. The universe is harmonious, not dissonant. A man is evil to the extent that he disrupts the natural order of things. He suffers without knowing it. In violating the equilibrium of nature, he violates himself. He is deprived of peace."

We walked along the cinder path. A boxer in training jogged towards us, jabbing the air. It was late afternoon. The water, unruffled by any breeze, reflected the clear lavender of the sky. A few smoky clouds lined the horizon, coasting above the skyline. The city across the reservoir gleamed in the last lambent rays of the sun. The reef, usually submerged, broke the surface of the water and supported a colony of gulls, all standing on yellow stick feet, looking south. No raucous cries filled the air. Noiseless jets like sharks slanted across the sky.

We walked at all hours of the day.

"Headley, would you say I am a virtuous person?"

"You are a silly goof," he said, putting his arm around me.

We approached the squat stone mansion belonging to the Department of Water Supply, an enormous piece of masonry with a dock into the reservoir. Two dories were tied to the dock, giving an impression of summer and tranquility.

"How about living here?" I asked Headley as we approached the edifice.

"Needs to be remodeled."

"Not too much. Just one big room."

"With no windows. A big dark room."

A man in khaki stood in the doorway. We peeked into the house and saw that it was unfit for human habitation. A ramp sloped into the water and brown barrels lined the walls.

"Four-hundred-pound barrels of copper sulfate to kill the algae," said the attendant. "The water comes down in mains from Croton, up the Hudson."

"Bit drafty," said Headley.

My only organized activity these days was walking in Central Park. Since the night of my communion with the luminous dial I had not heard from Al. That was more than three weeks ago. It was now mid-November. To distract myself and get my thoughts in order I took long walks in the park, sometimes alone, mostly with Headley, now and then with Abigail.

Abigail and I walked on Sundays on roads, closed to cars, teeming with cyclists. Our promenades offered a lot in the way of distraction but little in the way of rational dialogue. This state of affairs was due to Abigail, as my bent was increasingly cerebral. My emotions could be compared to a map of military maneuvers, each ambush and bivouac marked by a shifting series of pennant-headed pins. I traced my inner turmoil, figuring out the logistics of a campaign already lost, overseeing the plan of attack in an enclosure remote from the battlefield, sticking pins into past follies, charting the debacle. Abigail, who had predicaments of her own, preferred not to talk about matters of the heart. In her wholehearted way she complained and exclaimed about everything.

We walked at the side of the road, looking over the horde of bicycles as they were pedaled in our direction. Abigail made eyes at the more presentable male riders. In the course of our walk the same rider might tour the park two or three times, so he and Abigail could establish quite a rapport of winks and smirks. I was loftily indifferent to my fellow man, immersed in nature to the extent that one finds nature in a city park. My eyes found rest in the calligraphy of bare branches against the sky, the expanse of sky itself, and the open spaces of fields.

On one of our rounds, as we passed the ice-skating rink near West 107th Street and reached the summit of that hill, down which were racing members of the Bicycle Patrol in full regalia, a vile odor enveloped us.

"Phew," said Abigail. "Phew, phew. What is that revolting smell?"

"It smells like putrefaction. On days when the wind blows from New Jersey, it carries the smell of slaughtered pigs in Secaucus."

"Charming," she said, continuing to go "phew, phew" every few steps and making disdainful faces at the cyclists as though they were responsible for her olfactory distress.

We sat in the sun, were present at the scene of horseback accidents, were implicated in fleeting flirtations, and nodded at other bipeds like ourselves who ran at the side of the road, keeping in shape.

Abigail had an aversion to the wildlife. She hated pigeons and squirrels. Old ladies scattering bread crumbs to these denizens filled her with contempt.

"Verminous creatures," she said, referring to patron and patronized alike. "People are insane to allow pigeons to sit on their heads. They're disease carriers. As for squirrels, they're nothing more than rats with fancy tails."

"Sometimes rabid ones jump out of trees and land on your head. Then they take a good bite out of your ear," I said, contributing to our fund of animal lore.

Unlike Headley, Abigail was not concerned with muscle tone and didn't take walks for health reasons. She liked mingling with crowds. On days when the pollution was worse than usual she would work up a hatred of the air she breathed.

"Abigail, why are you making that extraordinary face?"

"It's a sneer. I'm sneering."

"At what?"

"At the air." A real city girl, Abigail liked crowds and distraction and felt less happy about exercise and silence.

Headley loved to hike and have his own thoughts. In this we resembled each other, driven to speech by necessity. Silence was our greatest point of contact. On our walks the train of thought would surface momentarily only to plunge, after an intake of oxygen, into the depths again. Our talk agitated the surface of our preoccupations like rain falling into a barrel of water.

26

Perimeter of the Eternal

MOZART APPROACHED the perimeter of the eternal with his opera *The Magic Flute*, a program note once informed me. Unable to grasp this concept I nevertheless applied it to our walks around the reservoir.

When we left the mansion and the attendant with his algae-demolishing copper sulfate, we fell silent. Earlier in the afternoon we were strolling along the bridle path taking in the equine scene when we became aware of a frantic galloping nearby. Few riders, however reckless, actually gallop. It is expressly forbidden. Some of the riders were accomplished equestrians, but most flapped around, bouncing off the saddle and yanking on the reins. In all cases, the gait never exceeded a slow canter, so at the sound of madly pounding hooves we pricked up our ears. Around the corner came a remarkable sight: a riderless horse, going at full tilt, head held high, stirrups and reins flying free.

Headley speculated on the fate of the rider but I tried to extricate myself from a bout of *déjà vu.* Where had I seen this runaway horse before?

It was in a dream. The horses in my dream, saddled and bridled but without riders, galloped along the paths of my mother's flower garden. They executed turns and reversals worthy of championship dressage, never trampling a single flower, relentless in their haste. When I awoke from this dream I understood its symbolism. Those riderless horses were my hopes.

There is a long stretch of path along the reservoir which is perfectly straight. Lampposts at the side lead the eye into the distance, precisely delineating perspective. The lamps and the wire mesh fence merge into a vanishing point. Out of this vanishing point now jogged a human form that looked shockingly like Al. Two seconds later I realized it was Al. I grabbed Headley. "It's Al. Let's get out of here."

"Why?" he asked in amazement.

Without another word, I jumped over the wire fence, not into the reservoir in a dramatic attempt to drown myself under Al's nose, but onto the grassy bank by the bridle path. I struggled through some bushes and hid behind a tree. Headley stood on the cinder path, looking indecisive. Peering around my tree, I saw Al approach. Headley stepped aside to let him pass. The two men glanced at each other blankly. When Al rounded the curve and disappeared I called to Headley. He worked his way through the bushes and came up to me, very annoyed.

"What kind of number is that?" he demanded.

"What do you mean, 'What kind of number?' " I retorted, angry and shaken. "I wasn't doing a number. I didn't want to see Al, that's all."

"That's not all, by any means. You don't jump over a fence and hide behind a tree simply because you don't want to see someone. You stay and say hello. Running into the bushes is erratic behavior, to say the least. And cowardly."

"Well, I am erratic and cowardly."

"Hilary, you're afraid of Al."

"Probably," I said, less sarcastically.

"And not just Al. You're afraid of confronting his reality with your illusions. There's no problem on a date. You can control the situation, to all intents and purposes. It's prepared in advance. But when you run into him like this you're on your own, and you can't face it. What kind of relationship is that? Why be so sad that it's over?"

"Headley, you're right. But please shut up now."

"Do we dare continue walking until we come to an exit? Or shall we vault over the wall onto the street?"

"Would you mind shutting up, Head?"

A man in the distance let his dog off the leash and the dog, a huge beast, took off in our direction. Goaded by some powerful impulse of friendship or enmity he dashed at us, his ears laid flat against his head.

"God, a Doberman pinscher. My least favorite dog. Are we being attacked?" I asked Headley. He took my arm and we both stopped. If Abigail were with us she'd be shouting, "Call off your dog."

The dog stopped too and raised his ears. His intentions remained inscrutable. His jaw hung open.

"I've never seen such a friendly attack dog," said Headley. "If he is friendly."

The owner was far away. He seemed to be calling his dog. Suddenly, the dog's hindquarters started wiggling. Since he couldn't wag his tail, having only a stub, he wagged his whole posterior.

"That looks friendly," I said. In a single bound he was fawning at our feet.

"A mutant," said Headley. "Highly erratic behavior."

"That makes two of us. He knows we have something in common, don't you, you awful dog," I said, trying to pat the dog's sleek head. The dog, fickle as well as erratic, ducked my caress and trotted back to his master.

"Friendly dogs and hostile ones both lay back their ears and wag their tails," declaimed Headley.

"Clever," I said. "Are you by any chance referring to me in some sneaky way?"

"My little paranoid," he said, taking my hand. "It refers only to dogs. Not to you. Not to Al. Only to dogs."

27

Farewell Dinner

We entered the bistro and stood waiting for a table, the object of everybody's idle attention. This particular place was a great favorite of Al's. There was a regular clientele, with-it and arty, and a subsidiary clientele of aspirants. People stared shamelessly and when you came in the front door you got it full blast. We had walked in many times as a couple. Tonight we entered as two people who happen to come in at the same time. Al spoke to the owner, with whom he was on chummy terms, and we were seated at the rear of the restaurant, running the gauntlet of eyes down the long narrow room before we reached our destination. I followed Al, eager to escape notice and to sit down as soon as possible. I wore a long cape and was imprisoned in its billowing folds. For too long,

I stood by the table, getting out of my cape. We sat down and watched the waiter lay the table.

Al was doing his duty tonight, taking me out for a good-by dinner. I had brought pressure to bear on his sense of honor, informing him in a letter that he had not behaved like a civilized person. The letter underwent numerous drafts and revisions, and the tone was lofty. Mistrusting the mails, I took it to his apartment and slipped it under the door. Rather bulky, it started to crumple. I eased it under as far as it would go. Al must have had trouble opening his door with that packet on the threshold. The next morning he called and asked me to dinner that evening. On the phone his tone was subdued and respectful. He humbly acknowledged my complaints, feeble as they were, and sounded anxious to see me. Although I knew it was a farewell dinner, like a testimonial for a retiring school librarian, my fancies at once flew out of hand, presenting me with the picture of a man who reads my letter, has a revelation and rushes out to buy an engagement ring. Any moment now, he would reach into his pocket and produce a little box.

"A friend of mine is here from London and is leaving tomorrow. I asked him to join us. I hope you don't mind."

"I don't mind."

In the last month Al had lost weight, bought contact lenses, spruced up his wardrobe, grown better looking as a result of these alterations, and infringed on his charm. I liked him chubby, bespectacled, and conventional. I had appreciated his opulence as long as it ran along conservative lines. Now that it extended to high male fashion, it was less successful. For someone else it might work. For Al, it was a mistake. He had too much brawn for adornment.

We had nothing to say. We cast our nets but failed to ensnare any conversational prey. Our nets were finely woven and easily torn, made expressly for the entrapment of small fish. To talk about our situation would be like attempting to net a whale. Afraid of falling into allusions of too intimate a nature and unable to prolong indifferent chatter, I sat and stared at people. Al stared too.

To our relief, Gregory showed up. British and sprightly, he introduced a lively tone. We jumped from topic to topic. Gregory and I did most of the talking. Al hunched over his food or leaned back in his chair, watching people table-hop. When he entered the conversation he addressed himself to Gregory. We tasted each other's dinners. Al speared a piece of roast veal and I ate it from his fork. He repeated the gesture with Gregory, who took the fork and fed himself.

After dinner the men ordered liqueurs. I asked for a sip of Al's Cointreau. I raised the glass to my lips and replaced it on the table but I set it on a wrinkle in the table cloth so that it fell over, spilling Cointreau into my lap and onto the skirt of a woman seated next to me.

Oh shit, is what, ordinarily, I would have said.

"Oh *no,*" was my present shriek of dismay. Gregory put his hand tentatively on my thigh.

"You didn't get too wet, did you?" he asked kindly.

"Are you all right?" Al asked the inundated lady beside me. "Sorry," he said, apologizing on my behalf. He reached across me and handed her a napkin. We stayed at the table another hour, drinking liqueurs. Al and Gregory smoked cigars. Gregory told us how he had been evacuated from a building that day during lunch because of a bomb scare.

"That's what you get for eating in capitalist places," said Al, laughing.

We talked about Women's Liberation. Even at this stage of the game, I was unable to attack Al as the direct cause of my present interest in Women's Lib, I discussed it theoretically rather than personally. Gregory said that the emasculators in the group, the real ball-breakers, were discrediting the Movement but, on the whole, he was moderately sympathetic. Al refused to take it seriously. "There's no way of insuring that an equal number of men get pregnant," Al said, drawing on his cigar and tilting back in his chair. The light from an unshaded lamp fixture on the wall cut across his face. His nose, straight and thin, caught the light like a blade. Aiming his nose at the waiter, he turned his profile to me, and in the reflex of stifling a yawn his nostrils flared disdainfully. That arc, slight as it was, conveyed a measure of boredom and vanity never apparent before. Tonight he was making no effort to charm me. I was a closed chapter. The little flaws and vanities, hidden until now, made their appearence for the first time. Far from taking satisfaction in fallen idols, I felt doubly abandoned. While it is one thing to be rejected by a man you love, it is quite another to be rejected by an impersonator.

28

Phony Accents

Gregory's brisk presence did much to leaven the loaf that Al and I had cooked up between us; a yeastless lump of dough, collapsed and sodden. Al had not briefed him, however, so he treated us like the young lovers we were emphatically not, giving us warm glances of approval. In the past, Al had seized every opportunity to pay me compliments in public. Now that Gregory supplied myriad launching pads, Al was at pains to disassociate himself from me, covertly but pointedly.

"Perhaps I should go and leave you children alone," Gregory suggested. "It's late."

"Why go?" asked Al.

"I, ahh, don't want to create friction."

Al smiled languidly. "You're not creating friction. Only electricity."

"I should get back to my hotel. My plane leaves early tomorrow. What are your plans for Thanksgiving, Al? Will you be going home?"

"Just for the day."

"Give my love to your admirable mother. Have you met Al's mother?" he asked me.

"No, but I've spoken with her on the phone." I quickly and noisily adjusted my chair hoping to distract attention from that ill-advised comment. It sounded like a sentimental reference to the past. We had long since exploited the sentimental potential of the past, using it to lay the foundations for sentiment in the present. Now we were demolishing the whole sentimental structure, such as it was, past and present. I regretted that slip about his mother.

Al was talking about his nieces.

"You have nieces? How could you when you're an only child?" asked Gregory.

"I'm not an only child. I have an older brother."

Gregory burst out laughing. "Don't come on avuncular, old boy. You and your nieces indeed. I've known you for ten years and never once have I heard about this brother."

"He's much older than I am."

"What does he do?"

"He works in the family business."

"Forgive me old fellow. It's been so long. What is your family business?"

"Bottle caps. We manufacture bottle caps," he said simply, issuing basic information about himself without revealing how he felt about the bottle cap business. He neither disowned his family's modest enterprise, nor took pride in it. Although he had come a long way from bottle caps himself, he remained loyal, if not precisely to bottle caps, certainly to his family. His loyalty took the form of secrecy. Al rarely mentioned his family but when he did, it was with affection and gratitude.

When we spoke of our childhoods I brought out the chaotic and repressive nature of mine, whereas Al emphasized the regularity and enlightened discipline of his. Comic books were a pivotal point. While my parents had not encouraged my consumption of comics, they condoned it with the result that many long afternoons of my early youth were spent acquiring an exhaustive store of specialized knowledge. Al had no such heritage. His parents forbade comics and maintained a high level of conversation at mealtimes. He and his brother and his parents matched wits in a healthy climate of competition.

The only meals I remembered were breakfasts when I had to sit in front of a heaping bowl of prunes until, by hook or by crook, they disappeared, and if the pits went too there was hell to pay because they alone proved the prunes had slithered down *my* gullet, not the dog's or the toilet's.

"When I go home people come up to touch me," Al told Gregory, comically plucking at his sleeve to show how somebody acquainted with the pudgy Cub Scout over two decades ago might reach out in awe to touch the meteor in its rise through High Finance and High Society.

I excused myself and went to the ladies' room, anxious to inspect the condition of my face. It seemed to me that, in spite of the spilled Cointreau and my slip about Al's mother, I had been holding up pretty well. I had responded with some zest to Gregory's timid chivalry, flirting with him in order to distract myself from Al. Al met my eyes only by mistake or in the course of a technical explanation which guaranteed an impersonal tone. Gregory, inserted between us, provided a logical excuse for our stiffness which would have been unbearable otherwise.

The bathroom was occupied. For a long time I stood outside the door, knocking and rattling the knob. Men passed to and from the men's room. No ladies joined me. The corridor was drab. Finally I gave the door a good bang. "Just a minute," came the familiar cry.

"It's been 'Just a minute' for an awfully long time," I hissed, not wishing to be overheard by the entire restaurant. A mascara-smeared, tear-streaked face peered around the door.

"Come on in," she said calmly. "Join the crowd."

The crowd turned out to be three disgruntled ladies putting on fresh applications of make-up. I squeezed my way into the tiny room and wondered what to do. The toilet itself was available but the mirror was not. The Three Graces, on the short side, did not fill the mirror all the way to the top. If I stood on tiptoe and loomed over them, a fragment of the glass would be mine. But this fragment and these overcrowded conditions were not what I needed. Opening my compact, I studied the features collected in the oval mirror. This strictly frontal view of my face gave me no clue as to my general appearance. Giving up, I left the ladies' room and returned to our table, less and less sure of my limited prerogatives.

Al suggested we go. The three of us rose and Al, near the wall, looked for our coats on the coat-rack.

"Is this yours?" he asked Gregory, holding up my cape, which he had seen me wear half a dozen times. Gregory pointed to his coat and Al handed it to him. He held mine in one hand and I stood before him waiting for him to lay it around my shoulders.

It is always the split second that counts. Like a child who carries a full bowl of soup and can't decide whether to walk with reckless assurance or painstaking deliberation and so stands still, gauging the slosh, I couldn't move to enable Al to help me on with the cape, nor could I decide to take it and put it on myself. I stood there, gauging the slosh. Usually careful about such niceties, Al dispensed with them now. He reached for his own coat and said to me, his face averted, "Take this." My hesitance annoyed him.

I never did manage to put on the cape. As we walked in single file to the door, stares filling the air like buckshot, I arranged the cape over my arm and carved out a moment of consciousness in which to be hurt. Al's grand apologies over the phone had been a sophisticated whitewash, a way of gaining control and the upper hand while, at the same time, testing me to see if I would press charges. Lacking resolute character, I had not pressed charges. I forgave him on the spot, giving him the option to go ahead and be a bully, which option he seemed to be taking. Gregory and I waited by the door while Al greeted some friends at a table. As he joined us he slapped one of the waiters on the back and said with a grin, "Lots of phony accents here tonight."

29

My Eyes Are Very Blue

In the car, sitting in the back, Gregory suddenly shifted into an uphill gear, lost his inhibitions, and roared full steam ahead.

"Don't mind me, you nice people up front. Pay no heed. Gregory is goofing off."

Al must have passed him the word that tonight was breakup night, for Gregory was greatly emboldened. He touched my hair and laughed whenever I said something that smacked of a joke. We drove to his hotel. On the way, Al and I competed for Gregory's attention and I won.

"How is your hotel?" asked Al, but he didn't get an answer because at the same time I demanded with great vivacity: "What do you eat for breakfast?"

"I have a delicious omelet, and grapefruit, and buttered toast, and, being English, tea," answered Gregory.

"No orange juice? I once paid a dollar for a glass of orange juice at your hotel."

"Good Lord. Well, look here, why don't you let me buy you a glass tomorrow morning? Come at nine o'clock. Do come. We'll have a smashing breakfast."

"Why don't you?" asked Al.

In a flash of anger at Al's way of handing me over to Gregory, I accepted the date, without any intention of keeping it, and gave Gregory my number and address. Al never showed signs of jealousy, perhaps because he was acquisitive rather than possessive. Unreconciled to the idea of personal loss, he attached himself only to replaceable commodities. Women fell into this category.

Gregory rollicked off into his hotel and we drove to my building. We didn't talk much on the way. It had rained during dinner. The sky was clear now but the pavements were wet and painted with reflected lights. Outside the range of windshield wipers raindrops quivered like pliant jewels. Al commented on the beauty of the city at night after a rain. He had made the same observation at other times. I was silent. Poor Al. It wasn't easy for him. But he had the satisfaction of behaving well in his own eyes. He drove alongside the curb and stopped the car. I got out and walked cautiously around to his side. When he locked the doors I knew he intended to come upstairs with me, which was more than I had expected.

While waiting for the elevator I asked the doorman for the house key. I had left mine in my apartment. He gave me the key on a large brass ring. In the elevator Al and

I noted the baronial dimensions of the key chain.

"Like a necklace," I said, trying to slip it on. The hoop was too small so I balanced it on the crown of my head, letting the key hang down between my eyes. "Modern jewelry," I smiled at him.

"Desdemona," he said, in a conditioned reflex.

"Would you like something to drink?" I asked when we walked into the sitting room.

"Do you have any wine?"

I brought in a bottle of red California wine, placed it on the table, and handed him a corkscrew.

"Could you open it? I can never work them."

"Don't you have any already open?"

"Some, but it must be vinegar by now. Go ahead. It's really not a treat." I forgot, and smiled. "Do you mind if I have orange juice?"

"Not at all."

I went to the kitchen, poured some orange juice into a wine glass, and walked back to the sitting room. I sat on the sofa as far away from Al as the pillows permitted, anxious to avoid any suggestion of old coziness. Kicking off my shoes, I brought my legs up and curled into the corner, waiting. He stretched his legs onto the coffee table, pushing aside a small philodendron plant.

"Are you comfortable?" I asked, impersonally, half lifting a throw pillow to place behind his head should he indicate that his comfort was incomplete.

Slouched on the sofa, he looked up furtively. "Fine."

"Your eyes are startlingly blue," I said.

"My eyes *are* very blue," he answered me.

30

It's Over

"My eyes are very blue," he said. Even the least vain of us knows the color of his own eyes but, at this moment, Al seemed positively entranced by his blueness. If he was so taken up with his blue eyes, this was going to be a lost cause. It occurred to me that except for the time when Al drove me home before driving to the airport, we had never seen each other outside in daylight. In the car I had marveled at his daytime face, admiring the fine-grained skin, the perpetual tan, even the new lines visible in the harsh light of day, and the tired blue eyes, caged in their glasses. For my part, I recalled, I had hidden my face with forward tosses of hair and quick movements away from his scrutiny. Face to face at stoplights I sought to rivet his eyes with my own and to dissuade him with smiles. Like a creature happiest in dark, sheltered places,

I tried to scurry away when the log was overturned. Human beings do not scurry away in observable fashion. They hold their ground and scurry away inside where nobody can see what is going on.

He supported the wine glass on his thigh, fingering the stem.

"You have an impressive literary style," he said, referring to my letter, by way of introduction.

"Thank you," I said, in voice an octave below its normal pitch. Some odd realignment was taking place in the membranes of my nasal cavity. My sinuses clicked involuntarily.

"As you know, I can be very uncommunicative," he continued in his slow, rather loud, humdrum way. "I believe in severing the umbilical cord. For me, our relationship was historical. Ten years . . ." He glanced up. Without an alleviating smile the bare eyes, small and intensely blue, had a dull, almost criminal, cast. The professional assassin.

Ten years was an exaggeration. It was only seven and a half.

"Every time I touched you I remembered the past. But it was a physical thing. I never loved you. For you it was different. I guess it is with women. They get involved more easily."

I nodded. I was trying, with the fingers of one hand, to braid the tassel of a throw pillow.

"I felt you spent too much time thinking about me. If you had stuck to your jobs . . . any kind of shit-eating job . . ."

"Al, it didn't work that way. Even when I had all three

jobs I still thought about you. When I'm drawn to someone . . ." I didn't know how to finish. He shrugged impatiently, looking into his lap.

"Drawn to someone," he repeated, with no particular emphasis. "But we weren't going anywhere." As a further gambit he added, "We never talked."

It was not my position to challenge the legitimacy of his decision to leave me. This was not a congressional debate. Forcing him to acknowledge he *had* left me, that it was not an oversight, a mere swing of the pendulum, was a major triumph. Although we had never really begun, at least we were ending with a bang. Even if I had arrogated certain rights to myself, beyond my right to an explanation, which I had already claimed, in my present state of feeling they hardly mattered. In a short time he would leave. Enumerating my violated rights, cogently portraying his misdemeanors, marshaling justifications and extenuating circumstances would serve no purpose. Besides, he wouldn't stand for it. Furthermore, I couldn't do it. The tassel was recalcitrant. I hunched into the sofa and had a picture of myself as a bedraggled bird.

"Why didn't we talk?" I asked, mashing the tassel.

"I don't know," he said.

At the time I wondered what he meant by *talk*. I wondered what he meant by "We weren't going anywhere." These reasons didn't ring true, but then I did not expect the truth. Enlightenment as to his precise reasons for dropping me was not what I sought, knowing full well that he had no reasons. He had drifted away, lured by a variety of better prospects, impelled by a sense of futility, resulting from a mixture of embarrassment and fear, experienced as boredom.

My motives were no less shabby than his reasons. Since I anticipated no satisfactory explanation, clearly I looked for something else from our meeting. I wanted to see him, to be with him, to win him back.

"I couldn't have told you this before," he said. "I couldn't have looked you in the eye. You have evoked more passion from me than any other woman, ever. Right now, my inclination is to take you over my shoulder, go into the other room, and seduce you."

"Don't," I whispered, meaning, "Don't say this."

"I won't," he said, misunderstanding me.

Although I had lost effective power of speech, I made inner objections to his Neanderthal image of throwing me over his shoulder, quite a feat, in any event, and one that we had never before attempted. The use of the word *seduce* also grated on me.

"You are not beautiful, you know," he informed me gratuitously.

"I know," I said. We sat still. "How did you know I thought about you? I tried so hard to conceal the fact."

Al shrugged.

"You have more intuition than I thought," I added. A second elapsed.

He placed his glass on the table, withdrew his legs, braced his hands on his knees, and said, prosaically, "*En tout cas* . . ." The summit meeting was being adjourned in French. "You suggested we remain friends. Well, friends . . . I dominate women. Always have." He leaned forward, about to rise. He got up and walked into the back room. I followed him like a polite hostess. On the hall table was an opera program.

"What opera did you see?" he asked, with that sweet, itemized interest in things that gave the false impression he cared about you and all the details, no matter how trivial, related to you.

"*The Magic Flute*."

"My coat. Where did I leave it?"

"Oh, it's in here. I'll get it." Walking quickly into the sitting room, I took it off the chair. Minutely conscious of time, I acted with dispatch, afraid of detaining him, making a mental equation between the flight of time and my measured response to it, as though time might take pity on me, rewarding me for keeping in step by granting me some unforeseen reprieve. If I lagged and bargained with it, I could expect no mercy. This was not the night for miracles, however. I held open his coat for him, like a coat-check girl, but he took it and put it on himself.

Parting was simple. Released from vague commitments to future dates, barred from the touches and assurances that redeem a separation from its overtones of finality, we just said good-by. Al said, "Good night," and after a moment's hesitation leaned forward to peck my cheek. I was unprepared for this gesture of conventional sociability. Having halted at an invisible boundary line, I was busy watching him take his leave across the hallway and was too far away to bridge the gulf. Unless I leaned towards him, the kiss would plant itself in thin air. We had to span a considerable distance. So, like two lovers on a Valentine's

Day box of candy, we stood upright and kissed cheeks perpendicularly.

"Good-by," I said.

He closed the door with a discreet slam. I had a last glimpse of a buckle on the sleeve of his trenchcoat. Walking into the sitting room, I looked at the depression in the sofa where he had sat, his wine glass, emptied, and the little philodendron plant which he had displaced. I leaned against the wall and thought, What am I going to do with my life now? I looked in the mirror to rediscover the color of my eyes but in the oblique light of the room no color appeared. There was only clarity in the illuminated segment of the iris, like a gelatinous arc with speckles. I picked up the necklace he gave me and hurled it to the floor, where the beads, glazed beans, scattered in all directions. Most flew off and rattled faintly under furniture. Some quivered near the ruptured strand. A few beans cracked open. I stared at them, and methodically, on hands and knees, collected the unstrung ornaments before going, much later, to bed.

31

She Didn't Play Me Right

"BUT WHAT did he say, Headley? Tell me exactly."

"He said you were stupid."

"Stupid?" It was a cold afternoon in early December. Heads lowered against the wind, hands jammed into pockets, intent on avoiding puddles, we trudged around the perimeter of the eternal, talking about Al.

"Stupid."

"Suppose we start from the beginning. Then we'll see what he meant by stupid. Stupid! God! I can't believe it."

"We were introduced at this party and I said, 'Al, oh yes, you know Hilary. Let me further introduce myself as Hilary's ex-almost-husband.' "

"You said that? Were you drunk?"

" 'Feeling no pain,' as they say."

"Begin again, Headley. All the details. Who gave the party, who was there, who was Al with . . ."

"I'm not a gossip columnist."

"I want a complete picture. Please try, Headley."

We were alone on our treadmill. The day was bleak beyond redemption. The waves in the reservoir splashed vengefully against the stone embankment and gulls rode the air currents, disconsolate. At the dock of the pump-house the dory was no longer afloat. Only the gunwales and the bow with its peeling bumper poked above the waves. Headley considered his narrative. I waited with a sensation akin to stage fright.

"The party itself isn't worth mentioning. It was given by an art dealer and his wife. Al came late, by himself, and left before I did. We met at the buffet table. At first he seemed uncomfortable in my presence but I, with my famous *savoir-faire*, set him at ease. Although a number of good-looking women wheeled by, he was politely indifferent to them, preferring to chat with me. He has a confidence in men that apparently does not extend to women. I must say, I found him charming. He didn't spend long sizing me up, assuming right off that we spoke in good faith and that I wouldn't spill the beans to you."

"He couldn't care less one way or the other," I said.

"That may be true. At any rate, the bastard you had described to me failed to materialize."

"Nobody's a bastard all the time.

Headley ignored this and went on. "While he spoke

forcefully enough, setting great store by his opinions, his deferential way of listening shows one of two things, or possibly both: either he has a real desire to learn or else he values other people's opinions more than his own."

I chose to comment on the less flattering possibility. "Because he doesn't have values, only opinions." I paused and gathered steam. "And he is prepared to defend those opinions with all the vigor of the weak, whose only real concern is to appear strong." I paused again. Having worked myself up to it, I delivered the final blow. "Because he doesn't have an ego, only vanity."

"Possibly correct," said Headley. "It's a bit unfair of me to leap to conclusions on the basis of a twenty-minute conversation. I was, on the whole, favorably impressed. He's a nice guy, likable, insecure, bright, but also a bit dense. He can't afford to forego people's friendship. He wants to be liked. You must have baffled him with your little games, which, by the way, were poorly chosen and badly executed. You played all the small games but not the one that counted with him."

"Namely?"

"Hard to get."

"I played hard to get."

"Not in the right way. You didn't demand his respect, according to him."

"What did he say?"

"He said, 'She's stupid. She didn't play me right.' "

"Conceited ass."

"If he *is* conceited it's about the wrong things. He has realistic accomplishments but seems ready to disavow them, to ply himself to other people's trades if they are momentarily more impressive than his own."

"He didn't ply himself to my trade."

"Your trade is pretty small potatoes."

"Headley!"

"From his standpoint, sex is inconsequential. Literally without consequence. It doesn't add up to anything."

"My trade is not sex, thank you very much."

"That's what you limited yourself to."

"I thought we had a tacit understanding."

"You had a tacit *mis*understanding, it would seem. You never bothered to map out the ground rules. In that respect, you were the conceited one, Hilary. What exempts you from exploitation? If you believe in yourself, you must insist upon extraordinary treatment."

"I wanted ordinary treatment, that's all."

"Well, you got it."

"Cynic."

"And Al is an idealist? You misread his character. I base my evaluation of him on intuition and on knowledge of similar types. His density is self-induced. It results from looking in too many directions at once. His antennae are out, he receives many signals, but the wavelengths are too profuse. They get intercepted. The message that ultimately gets broadcast on his inner radio is either garbled or static. If it is garbled, he adjusts the tuning knob. If there is static, he switches stations. When he switches stations what he hears is a propaganda speech."

I had to laugh.

"Look, angel," said Headley, softening, "men fall in

love each according to his character. I have no sense of time and am both irascible and mystical which makes me an ideal candidate, from a woman's point of view, if I may say so. Al, on the other hand, has an overdeveloped sense of time and tremendous physical energy which makes him the ideal hit-and-run lover."

"How elegantly you put it."

"Don't get sarcastic. I don't discount your abundant charms. But your true charms lie deeper than Al was prepared to venture."

"Poor thing. Think what he missed."

"You are not beautiful, you know."

"It's a conspiracy! I swear it's a conspiracy."

"What's a conspiracy?"

"Al said the same thing. I've never thought of myself as a beauty queen but, all the same, it's not music to my ears to be told I'm ugly."

"Who says you're ugly? You're beautiful."

"It's a variable, huh?"

"You have a mobile face that reflects what you feel. Your expression is interesting, changeable. Feature by feature you are not, strictly speaking, beautiful. If your nose were placed in a row of other noses, I daresay your nose, by itself, would not emerge victorious."

"Leave my nose out of it."

"Noseless, your face would not be enhanced." We laughed. Headley took my arm. "We say you are not beautiful when forced to resist your charms or because we want to make it clear you are not unique as we think you are."

Headley thought a moment. "To play him right, as he put it, presupposes a coldness that is quite beside the point if the point, for you, is love. It's simple enough to manipulate someone if you don't give a damn about him. If you care, the best you can do is to play yourself right."

"Headley," I asked, after a little while, "do you think many women fall for him?"

"Insecure women who feed on his insecurities in order to feel strong themselves."

"Like me?"

"Like you. A strong woman wouldn't put up with his nonsense."

32

Late Bloomer

IT WAS the Christmas season and everyone was going someplace. Abigail had been offered a position on the editorial board of a fashion magazine with offices in Paris and had accepted the new job, tempted by the prospect of life in a foreign capital. She was flying to Paris for Christmas. We had already exchanged gifts and said good-by.

Headley had booked passage on a freighter sailing for North Africa. He maintained that Christmas had no special meaning for him and he would probably pass it in the mid-Atlantic.

I was going home, to become a child again. By this time I should have reached the final stages of acceptance but I was still groping in the dark. Al was gone forever. He was gone, but what about my feelings, which still trailed behind him like confetti streamers, the shreds of an old celebration? It was Christmas time and, in the same old pattern of hanging around, I was going home again, as a child.

My mother said to me once, after a fight, "No matter how old and smart you get, you're still my child. You'll always be a child to me."

I was going home, a twenty-five-year-old child. Where had Al left me?

"You're a late bloomer, dear," my mother had consoled me, "you come from a long line of late bloomers." I could see the family tree, blooming in its own arbitrary spring, wizened faces wreathed in youthful smiles, the sap running high in shriveled limbs. But my bloom had come and gone. In Al's sunshine I had bloomed and now the bloom was gone. I was ripe and ready to be picked and I hung on the bough, uselessly mature.

Headley paid me a last visit before his departure. I gave him a small package and made him promise to wait until Christmas before opening it. He gave me a paper bag filled with rattling lumps. I took the bag and peered within. Half a dozen gourds greeted my eyes. With all due ceremony I said: "Oh." Headley and Al, dissimilar in every respect, somehow came up with similar earthy gifts. A necklace of beans. Six great desiccated squash.

"You hate them," said Headley.

"No, I don't."

"You do."

"I don't hate them."

"Be honest."

"I just can't bear them," I blurted out. We both laughed.

"Let's have a good look," he said, taking the bag. He removed the gourds, one by one, lining them up on the table. Some were smooth and shellacked and resembled cucumbers. Others were misshapen and multicolored and looked like troubled melons.

"The only good squash is a dead squash," said Headley.

"Are they dead? I don't understand them. A dead squash is a live gourd, is that how it works? The way a dried grape is a raisin?"

"Gourds are members of the squash family. They have a hard shell and a pulpy inside but are quite inedible. Hollowed out, they serve as utensils. Otherwise, their sole function is to exist as an artifact."

"Do they die?"

"Not exactly. They aren't prone to death because they have no real life inside. They just kind of perish. In fact, some of these are already beginning to rot. They're out of season."

We glared at the gourds. In some way, I wanted to clarify my sense of inner nullification by relating to these obdurate squash, but the more I thought about the gourds, examining them, holding them in my hand like Yorick's skull, the more I felt we had nothing in common.

I was a fruit, bloomed and thin-skinned. I was neither an inedible artifact nor an eviscerated utensil. My life was wholly within me. Headley wasn't a gourd either. His tendrils were fresh and seeking, not brittle wisps. Abigail was in no sense a member of the vegetable kingdom and therefore would never qualify, by any stretch of the imagination, as gourdlike.

But the gourds had a place in my existence.

"Headley, they haunt me. Would you be terribly hurt if I threw them out?"

"Let me do it. They're frightening. I don't know why I bought them in the first place, or why I thought they'd fascinate you."

"They fascinate me all right. But I'd prefer something I could live with. Like flowers."

"Cut flowers die so soon. You arrange them in a vase and have the pleasure of watching them die more every day."

"O.K. A plant then."

"Excellent idea. What kind?"

"Something that lasts."

"For Christ's sake, Hilary. Nothing lasts. If you want something technically alive that persists, keep the goddamned gourds."

"But they scare me."

"Make up your mind. What is it you want?"

"I want . . ." I looked at Headley, who watched me sternly, with his no-nonsense face.

". . . To go live on a farm in Saskatchewan."

"Unacceptable."

"I want. . . What do I want, Headley?"

"Yourself."

"Myself . . . Can you give that to me for Christmas?" I asked, jokingly.

His eyes softened under lifted brows. Swiftly, he brushed my forehead with his mustache, gathered up the gourds, and turned to go. At the door he said:

"Give it to yourself, angel. Take the risk, and give it to yourself."